Twists of Fate

(Tales of Hope)

by

Jonas Saul

PUBLISHED BY:

Imagine Press Inc.
Ebook ISBN: 978-1-927404-63-8
Paperback ISBN: 978-1-998047-92-5
Hardcover ISBN: 978-1-998047-91-8

Twists of Fate (Tales of Hope)
Copyright © 2021 by Jonas Saul

The Sarah Roberts Series

Dark Visions (One)
The Warning (Two)
The Crypt (Three)
The Hostage (Four)
The Victim (Five)
The Enigma (Six)
The Vigilante (Seven)
The Rogue (Eight)
Killing Sarah (Nine)
The Antagonist (Ten)
The Redeemed (Eleven)
The Haunted (Twelve)
The Unlucky (Thirteen)
The Abandoned (Fourteen)
The Cartel (Fifteen)
Losing Sarah (Sixteen)
The Pact (Seventeen)
The Terror (Eighteen)
The Chase (Nineteen)
The Betrayal (Twenty)
Sarah's Return (Twenty-One)
The Hunt (Twenty-Two)
The Delivery (Twenty-Three)
The Trap (Twenty-Four)
The Ultimatum (Twenty-Five)
The Depraved (Twenty-Six)
The Condemned (Twenty-Seven)
Payback (Twenty-Eight)
The Unknown (Twenty-Nine)
Wrath (Thirty)
The Damned (Thirty-One)

Jonas Saul

The Game (Thirty-Two)
The Decoy (Thirty-Three)
The Disappearance (Thirty-Four)
The Whole Truth (Thirty-Five)
Alex (Thirty-Six)
Parkman (Thirty-Seven)
Darwin (Thirty-Eight)
Aaron (Thirty-Nine)
Remains To Be Seen (Forty)

The Jake Wood Novels

The Immortal Gene (Book One)
The Immortal Target (Book Two)

Standalone Novels

'Til Death Do Us Part
The Drowning
The Woman in the Woods
The Threat
The Specter
The Mafia Trilogy
A Murder in Time
Frequency of the Dead

Co-Authored Novels

Collision Course (Written with Gary Ponzo)
There Will Be Blood (Written with Rania Stone)
The Soulless (Written with Rania Stone)

Short Story Collections

Twisted Fate (Tales of Horror)
Twists of Fate (Tales of Hope)

The Newspaper

I CAN'T BELIEVE I'M sitting in my car, waiting for someone I don't know, staking out an accident scene that hasn't happened yet.

I'm hoping to save these people, even though they are meant to die, or maybe it's fated to die. I'm pretty sure it will happen. Strange, I know, but I must wait this out as my conscience won't let me leave.

It all started yesterday morning when I woke up. I made my usual coffee, opened the blinds to let in the sunshine, and went to the front door, where I collected my morning newspaper from the welcome mat, pulling it from its protective plastic bag. I settled in the living room and browsed the paper while sipping my morning medicine.

Nothing unusual is happening in the news. All the same bad shit, but hey, I'm addicted to the news.

Then, a funny item on the second page caught my attention. It was a story about a woman and her three teenage daughters, all killed by a large truck in the parking lot of a hotel where the traveling psychic fair was currently being held.

It caught my eye because of the irony. I mean, didn't they see it coming? I'm not trying to belittle the fact that these four people are dead. That was my first thought, as morbid as it was. I finished reading the newspaper—and my coffee—without any more derogatory thoughts about society's senseless violence and general meanness. Although, I did have a few select words in mind when I saw my favorite hockey team had lost another game.

The rest of my day went without incident. Not that my days generally go by with any kind of excitement. I'm a sixty-five-year-old skeptic and proud of it. I help around the local golf course as a course marshal in the summers and dilly-dally my winters away.

I should probably add that the only thing I do religiously is read the morning newspaper every day. I can't miss one, and I don't miss one—ever.

This morning, I woke up and turned on my coffee machine like every other day. I got the newspaper from the porch and started my morning ritual. A blurb on the front page announced that the psychic fair was in town and was opening its doors at noon.

Noon?

Confused? Well, so was I. How could that be? The fair had started yesterday. I'd read about the woman and her three daughters dying on the first day of the psychic fair.

It had to be an error. Boy, won't someone be paying dearly for that kind of typo?

I continued reading my paper. Nothing else terribly important caught my attention. As I was closing the paper and folding it for the recycle box, I saw the advertisement for the psychic fair again and decided to reread it. As plain as day, the printed words stated that the fair would be underway at noon today.

If that was the case, then what did I read yesterday? Maybe it said the four women were killed a day before the beginning of the fair, and I'd just missed it. That would surprise me because I usually don't miss those kinds of details. I distinctly remember commenting on how they hadn't seen it coming.

I ambled out to the garage and yanked yesterday's paper from the recycle box. I opened it to the second page and felt my eyes bulge. My grip tightened on the edges of the newspaper. I looked left, right, up, and down. I turned the pages back and forth. There was no mention of the women killed in yesterday's newspaper.

I couldn't believe it. I still don't believe it.

I stood in my garage, going over every detail. I remembered it said the fair had commenced to tragedy. Four women were killed in a freak accident that had caused an explosion. Something about a transport truck losing control, hitting them, or hitting their parked car. When it happened, the four women were the only ones in that part of the parking lot. It even named the hotel where the psychic fair was being held. How could I know that if I hadn't read it yesterday? Especially since I don't believe in any of that mumbo jumbo.

I wondered if I was losing my mind. Could I have dementia? Or had I seen the future?

So, because I have a strong belief in what I read in yesterday's newspaper—I'm anal like that—I drove out to the hotel where the psychic fair is being held and parked near the section where the accident was supposed to happen, or better yet, is supposed to happen. I don't know what the women look like, though, as the newspaper didn't provide that handy detail. I don't know what I will do or how I will do it. In fact, I feel stupid and clueless.

And now, the fair had started thirty minutes ago, and several people have come and gone in the hour I've been here.

There has been no vehicle with four females yet.

I check the clock on my dashboard and consider the levels of my stupidity. Oh, the heights we aspire to at times.

When I check the parking lot one more time, an old Pinto pulls in and angles into a parking spot backward. Its tail end is a few feet from the highway, with a small grassy area separating its bumper from the gravel shoulder. The Pinto doors open, and four women step out.

"Here we go," I whisper. "This has to be them."

I open my door and shamble toward them in my lame ability to walk with a sore hip that I've honed over six decades.

A Pinto makes sense since everyone knows those cars are bombs when hit from behind due to the unfortunate placement of the gas tank.

The only information I had about the women was that they comprised a mother and her three daughters.

Walking toward them, I realize how crazy this is. But if I'm wrong, no harm done. If I'm right and didn't act on my suspicion, these four women would be in tomorrow's newspaper.

"Excuse me," I say as I hustle closer, my arm raised. "May I ask you a question?"

They look at each other and then back at me. One of the daughters seems to be having trouble breathing. She gasps twice and stumbles into her sister. I'd typically ask if she was okay, but more pressing matters are at hand.

The woman who looks the oldest tells me to go ahead and ask my question.

"This will sound strange, but are the four of you related? I mean, are you a mother, and these are your daughters?"

My stomach is flipping. This could be classified as the stupidest thing I've ever done. If they were to ask why I needed to know and I told them the truth, they would think I'd lost my mind.

I look over my shoulder and scan the two-lane highway for any big rigs barreling our way. Even though sweat has broken out on my forehead, I'm relieved not to see any.

"You know," the mother says. "It's pretty lame that you would ask us questions in the parking lot before getting our readings done. Tell your fake psychics that they won't be able to wow us with knowledge about our family status because we're not going to tell you shit, old man. Our readings aren't authentic if the psychic doesn't know what's what. End of story."

All four women walk away from me. This was now in my top three for the most embarrassing things I've ever done

(I will not reveal the other two here).

I would never have imagined they'd take me for a psychic's aid, attempting to glean information from people before they entered the fair.

Dejected, I turn around and head back to my car. I guess I was wrong. The psychic fair has started. There have been no accidents and no explosions. I figure I'll stick around for ten more minutes and then head home.

I stare at the clock on my dash again and change my mind.

"I'm leaving now. That's it. I'm outta here."

I start the car, put it in gear, and drive toward the exit. With one final glance over my shoulder, I see everything's fine. My foot presses the accelerator, and I merge onto the two-lane highway.

That's when I see the rig.

In my rearview mirror, one of the three teenagers is running behind my car, waving her arms frantically.

What's that about?

I looked forward again. Half a kilometer ahead, the large tanker truck wobbles back and forth.

I apply the brakes. The truck swerves into oncoming traffic and knocks what looks like a Buick off the road. The rig continues on its path toward me.

I got my vehicle stopped. Then, I performed a U-turn to head back toward the hotel's parking lot.

All four women are now standing on the edge of the road, waving at me.

"What the hell are you doing?" I shout at them, even though they can't hear me. "Get the hell out of the way.

Don't let the prophecy come true."

The truck is gaining fast. The driver must have problems with his brakes to be gaining like that. If he'd fallen asleep, he'd have woken up by now.

To my horror, the four women are now running toward their Pinto.

I lay on my horn as I enter the parking area—my window protests as I lower it using the old windup handle.

"Get out of the way!" I shout, then choke on my saliva. "Move away from your car—"

I'm still fifty yards from the women when they slow their steps. I know they saw me waving my arm out the window. At that second, they must've taken me for a nutcase, yet they continue to jog as a group toward their car. I can't believe what I'm seeing. I now tear my eyes away from them and watch the rig amazingly close in my rearview mirror. The driver has tried to slow it down by steering the rig onto the shoulder and the grass, digging up the earth as he goes, and using the softer ground to ease the speed.

I then realized that what I had read yesterday was tomorrow's newspaper. If the truck driver can't put his rig back on the highway, he will hit the line of parked cars, starting with the Pinto.

None of us will escape the ensuing tragedy.

It's my last chance to do something useful. I aim my car at the women and lean my elbow into the horn.

I'm screaming, too, my heart racing.

But now I have their attention. I'll hit these women if they don't stop running and turn back toward the hotel in seconds.

That's the defining moment, that one decision.

Left or right, life or death.

All four of them turn at the same time. I don't know if it was because they thought I'd completely lost my mind and was trying to run them down, or maybe as a group, they finally saw the transport truck bearing down on them and recognized the danger that I was attempting to avert.

***

The next day's newspaper had the same information on the second page that I had read two days prior. Some of the details were different now, though. All four women were unhurt. No one died in the accident. Two people were sent to the hospital with non-life-threatening injuries—the truck driver and me.

The Pinto blew up, and the shockwave knocked out my car's back window. A large chunk of glass made a home in my shoulder. Other than a wicked scar, I'll be fine.

My first night in the hospital was painful. I couldn't sleep well with my injury throbbing like it was. Where did I get the idea that I was Steve McQueen come back to life? The brutal act I performed to save strangers wasn't heroic; it was stupid.

Sure, I'm happy everyone made it out okay. My actions weren't fruitless, but I could spend the rest of my life not doing anything remotely close to what I did yesterday, and I'd be fine with that.

My hospital room door opens, and an old woman enters. She turns and quietly closes the door behind her. The sun's high enough in my window to shine on her entire body. I can tell right away she isn't a nurse. As far as I can figure, she probably has the wrong room.

"Can I help you?" I ask, the pain rising at the use of my voice.

She turned and faced me, both hands clutching her large handbag suspended in front of her waist.

She doesn't say anything at first. She just moves closer until she's standing at the end of my bed. I don't talk again because it's too painful. So I wait.

A tear springs to her eye. She wipes it. "So, this is what you look like."

What the hell does that mean? Taken literally, what could I look like if not myself?

"What?" I manage, then grimace.

"After all these years, you still look good. I've really missed you."

Okay, bizarre, I don't like, odd, I don't mind, but fucked up is fucked up.

Walking inside my hospital room and acting like you know me, dropping compliments, and expecting me to rejoice in our reunion without the obligatory getting-to-know-you shit leads me to the question: what side are your crackers salted on?

"Do I know you?" I ask. It's lame, but it's all I've got at the moment.

She nods.

"Great. Since I know you, I'm pleased to meet you." I grimace again.

There, I'm being polite, all the while adding to my pain by talking. At least the pain is in my shoulder and not my ass.

If this woman doesn't start explaining things, the pain will soon be in my ass.

"We met a long time ago. I've looked long and hard for you."

I frown, still clueless. And now I don't want to talk anymore.

The woman seems to be about my age. She's easily in her sixties. Maybe Alzheimer's has gotten to her. Perhaps some other mind-altering ailment has befallen this old woman. I chuckle inside at the notion that I was calling her old when I'm probably older than she is.

She moves along the bed and stands beside me. I'm unsure if I should grab the button thingy to call the nurse or wait to hear what the woman wants.

"You don't remember me, do you?" she asks.

I slowly roll my head back and forth along the pillow, careful of my shoulder injury.

She touches the sheets on the bed. "How did you know about Margaret and her daughters? How could you know?"

"I don't know anything. You are a confused person." I wince and decide I really need to stop talking.

"The summer of 1965. We were both twenty years old. Do you remember the fair that came to town that June?"

I push my head back into the pillow but can't escape. This woman is talking nonsense. Summer of '65? Fair in town? Ancient times. I'd been married and widowed since then. No kids. Lived a full life. And now I've got an old woman in my hospital room talking stupid shit. Woe is me.

She scans the room. Her head stops at the chair by the window. She walks over, grabs it, and sits it beside my bed.

After settling in, she says, "Oh, Michael, didn't we have a great time that summer?"

I might add that I had a lot of great summers with a few different girls. There was one girl, though, but … Nah, it couldn't be.

"Do you remember taking me to the drive-in theater when it opened? The memories of that summer never left me. I had to leave for school in September. Can you remember what you gave me as a going-away present?"

My hallway of memories has many doors. I can almost feel the old, broken down, and musty doors unlocking themselves as they slowly open and allow me to rummage through their contents.

Things began to click in place.

Jackie Stevens.

The love of my life.

The girl who I thought would be my wife one day. We fell in love instantly. Then she left me. I never heard from her again. It didn't help that my parents moved us away right after school started that year.

But no, this couldn't be. There's no way in hell this is Jackie Stevens.

The woman that I compared all future women to. God rest her soul—my wife and I had a glorious relationship. She was like Jackie in many ways. There was always a tiny spot in my heart for the Jackie I knew at twenty. I used to think of it as history. She was there because there was a history. Thinking about her now, I realize there's always a spot in my heart for Jackie because I always have, and always will have, loved her to the ends of the earth. My Jackie Stevens, the one woman I could never find after that summer.

Could this woman know something about Jackie, or was she saying she was Jackie? The Jackie?

"I left you that summer with a special present," the old woman continues. "I was pregnant with Margaret, who became Margaret Stevens. She grew up and had three daughters herself." The woman stops to wipe her eyes. "How did you know?"

Was she saying what I thought she was saying? There's no way in hell. Right?

"The four women I saved yesterday …"

The woman nods.

"… are related to me?"

She nods again.

"Margaret is my daughter, and the three girls in their late teens are my granddaughters?"

The woman nods once more, wiping at more tears streaming now.

"I married in my twenties and never had any more kids. My husband died a few years ago. I started looking for you again but came up empty-handed. Margaret has always wanted to meet her real father. I told her wonderful stories about how kind you were. Everything I could remember. Then you pop up out of nowhere and save their lives. It's a miracle, Mike, a miracle. A true piece of heavenly intervention."

I refuse to believe what she's saying. But the more I stare at her, the more I can tell she's Jackie. The slope of her cheek, the look in her eyes. I'd stared into them long enough all those years ago.

The hospital door opens. The women I saved yesterday, my family, enter and step up to the bed. I feel lost at sea, drifting into a familiar but unknown reality. The youngest girl held a newspaper. She holds it up for me to see.

It was the same paper from two days ago. The one I had read showed them all dead in the parking lot of the psychic fair.

"I saw you," she said. "On page two."

"I saw you, too," I respond before I can stop myself.

"The paper said," the girl continues, "that my grandfather would be in an accident in the parking lot of the psychic fair. I dragged my mom and sisters there so we could meet you. I didn't tell them anything. Only that I had a lead on where you'd be. After you approached us in the parking lot, it took me a few minutes to compose myself, then convince them to turn around and find you before you had your accident or left the area." She stops and looks down at the paper. "When I turned back to page two, everything I had read was gone, as if it was never there in the first place."

I nod. "That happened to me, too. Exactly as you describe it, minus the family connection part."

"Oh, Michael," Jackie says. "I've missed you all my life."

"It's nice to meet you finally, Dad," Margaret says.

The hugs irritate my shoulder wound, but I don't mind.

I'm crying because of the pain.

Truly, I am.

The pain of loss and wounds.

I have a family now. An act of God blessed me.

I'm also a believer. The skeptic has left the building.

***

Afterword

This story was entered into the 75th Writer's Digest Annual Short Story Contest in 2007 and placed in the 6th position out of almost 20,000 entries. For that year, I won a copy of the book Writer's Market and my first-ever check for writing something ($25.00).

This story is also dear to my heart as it's about two things I love—the other side and family.

I have a large family—seven brothers and sisters. We grew up in a terrible time, struggling as many families do. To this day, I'm still in contact with one sister, and that's only a couple of times per year. Two of my brothers are dead, my mother has passed away, and I have no idea where the rest of my siblings are.

People drift apart and move on, and while all that was happening, I was always pro-family, but it didn't work out with blood.

I've found my family in the people I have in my life.

I've found my love in the acceptance and understanding of my woman, our cute little family, and my two daughters' eyes.

I'm in my fifties, still read my paper, and drink coffee in the morning.

I've experienced several psychic events, with two of them inspiring the Sarah Roberts Series, which I went on to write after these short stories.

Some things never change.
Onward and upward …

Near Death Experience

THE LOVE OF MY life died last week.

I didn't even get to meet her.

It all started on a lark. I joined an online chatroom four months ago. After a few days, I talked to a happy, positive woman. We immediately hit it off, exchanged email addresses, and started a day-to-day conversation. Our online dates escalated to a romantic level. I sent roses to her office building and mailed twenty-seven birthday cards for her birthday. Each one represented the years I hadn't met her yet —the years that finally brought us together.

Yet, the whole time, I still felt something was missing. Not missing in the sense of what the relationship offered me, missing in the sense that she wasn't telling me something. Like she was married, or maybe she was a man—which would suck. This undiscussed thing made me feel I couldn't completely trust her.

My sleep began to suffer from thinking something wasn't quite right. After several months of online dating, she still hadn't told me the one thing she was holding back, even though I knew there was something. I could tell the extra pause before answering questions by the words she chose. She was reserved, cautious, and careful—even when she seemed evasive.

Initially, I had no intention of getting involved in an online romance—I'm a writer, and at the beginning, I was simply collecting information for a novel. I used to be the guy who wondered about the social skills of people who met others online. Why couldn't they meet the old-fashioned way? I wanted to get insight into the chatroom fad.

I had no idea I'd fall in love.

But now she's dead.

Andrea had been a blessing. She opened areas of my heart I didn't even know I had. Writers are loners. We sit by ourselves and develop our craft. I had no idea how alone I was until I met Andrea.

I read in the newspaper about a murder the police had responded to on the other side of the city. I read the name of the deceased.

It was my Andrea.

Next of kin had been notified. Her boyfriend was in custody.

I finally found out that was the information she was hiding from me. She had an abusive boyfriend, and I was probably her way out.

According to friends and relatives, her boyfriend had a

history of abuse. She had been in the process of leaving the relationship. I became someone she was excited about again. Somehow, I inspired hope in her. She once called me her savior.

I was devastated when I found out she had been killed.

The last email I received from Andrea confirmed a meeting place. It would have been the first time we were to meet in person. Neither one of us had ever sent a photo. We'd used descriptions in our correspondence but never pictures.

We had agreed to show up at the coffee shop and try to find each other. A sly smile, a nervous twitch in the stomach, shuffling of the feet, and then a warm hello. Both of us were super nervous about meeting the other.

Out of respect to Andrea, the woman I was and still am in love with, I decided to go to our prearranged meeting place anyway to honor her memory.

I sat alone with the coffee I had just ordered. It tasted like dishwater and had a peculiar smell to it. I held it and glanced through the large window to my left. Cars whizzed by. Life went on without Andrea.

I started to cry. I think it was the loneliest moment of my life.

So, I whispered a silent prayer for Andrea.

How could the world be so cruel?

The door chime made my head turn. A woman walked in, scarves wrapped around her neck and lower face. Something about the woman held my attention. The first scarf came away, and our eyes locked. I saw her bruised face and purple splotches surrounded by yellowing areas.

For a heartbeat, I wondered if this was Andrea.

Wouldn't that be something? Back from the dead.

Another scarf came away. More bruising around the neck. She watched me as much as I was watching her for some reason. Her eyes, her facial structure—a captivating beauty for sure.

I looked back at the cars on the street to wipe my eyes. My coffee was getting cold, but I didn't care. It tasted like shit, anyway.

When I turned back, the woman was about to sit on the empty chair at my table. I leaned away, startled.

"Can I help you?" I asked, befuddled. "Do I know you?"

She smiled, and I felt my heart flutter.

"I saw you when I died," she said.

I didn't know what to say. I knew it couldn't be Andrea since she was dead, so who was this woman? No one knew why I was there so that it couldn't be a joke—I wasn't being punked or pranked or whatever the fuck they called it. I had read her obituary and knew Andrea was dead.

"Who are you?" I asked.

"Andrea," she whispered.

I nearly fainted on the spot. What kept me upright was the shock of her statement.

"But … that's not possible. How could it be?" I tilted my head and took her in. Was I talking to the dead? Since I'm not into new-age religion, I dismissed that idea. I've never even seen a ghost.

"My death wasn't permanent. It's what they call a Near Death Experience."

She went on to explain how she died. I sat in rapt fascination, my stomach clenching and my hands twitching.

The writer in me wanted to jot everything down, but I resisted, lest it be construed as rude.

She said that her vital signs had ceased. When she woke, she found that a blanket—which rose and fell to the soft rhythmic caress of her breathing—had been placed over her body.

"I saw you," she said again.

I wasn't ready to talk much yet, so all I said was, "How?"

"When I died. I saw you writing on a laptop. You looked at peace, relaxed as you typed."

I didn't know what to say. I usually have words at my disposal, but she had rendered me speechless.

"I saw something else," she added.

I waited to see if she'd reveal this other tidbit, still not finding more than one-word replies in my mouth.

"I saw you save me."

So cryptic. If love had levels, mine shot several stories at that moment.

"Save you?" I seemed to have found my voice. How could I save her?

"Yes, save me. And I love you for it, Max."

She leaned forward, stared into my eyes, then kissed me.

I let her.

After all, this was Andrea, the woman of my dreams, the woman I had fallen in love with, back from the dead, talking about how I saved her.

How the hell did I pull off that feat?

The least I could do was accept a kiss, even though I felt lost. I was stunned and utterly flabbergasted that Andrea wasn't dead. Questions raced through my mind. Why hadn't she emailed me in the past week if she'd been alive all that time? What if I hadn't come to the coffee shop? Could there be even more secrets? Was she someone I could trust?

Our lips parted as the door to the coffee shop banged open, the door chime almost ripping off. I jumped at the sound of the door, me being a bundle of nerves and all, and turned to see a tall man enter. He looked angry, eyes wild, breathing rapidly.

He stared at us. I stared back. He wore a black leather jacket and some kind of biker pants. A black goatee clung to his chin, and a long tattoo of a scythe circled his ear and dropped down along his neck. He looked mean. He looked angry. But most of all, the violence on his face made my bowels loosen.

I wasn't the only one who noticed that this man didn't look like a paying customer. The guy behind the counter stepped back and touched the phone. Maybe it was the clenched fists, the red face, or maybe the man's low moan that made the coffee shop worker hold the receiver in his hand.

Then the man screamed Andrea's name.

He stormed over to our table and looked down at me. I thought for a quick second that he would wind up and punch me. I was surprised that my underwear didn't need to be changed yet.

"Colin, you're not supposed to be here," Andrea said. "I have a restraining order. Please, Colin, just leave before something bad happens."

He turned to face her. "Fuck you, you fucking whore. How dare you fake your own death. Thought you could get away from me? Well, I've got news for you." He jabbed a thumb my way. "Who's the asshole? He better be a long-lost brother or give you a job interview."

Colin was shouting now. I was more scared than I'd ever been or than I'd care to admit. I'm a writer. I write these kinds of things. I don't act them out.

"Get up," Colin ordered. "Now. We're leaving." He reached for Andrea's arm but missed. She'd pulled back far enough to avoid his grasp.

A red and blue flashing light registered in my peripheral vision.

Good, the coffee shop guy had called the police.

The biker saw it, too. In a deep guttural grunt, he shouted at the clerk, "I'll be back to deal with you."

He reached out far enough to get Andrea. He pulled her out of the booth with massive strength and into a standing position. She squealed and tried to wiggle out of his hand clamp.

I had no idea what I was doing. I looked back and tried to reason why I would do it in the first place. Rationally, I know why, but I remain puzzled on every other level of my being.

My foot swung out. I grabbed the edge of his jeans and gave him a sharp tug. This caught him off balance. He fell backward over my outstretched leg, his hands releasing Andrea as he pinwheeled his arms on his way to the floor.

I grabbed my coffee, still somewhat warm on the outside of the cup, and flung it in his face.

He roared like a bear, shook his face to clear his vision, and jumped back to his feet like his name was Jack and someone had wound his little box.

The cop car stopped out front. I would be dead in four seconds. They would arrive in ten, so much for bravery.

Andrea had moved away from him. She stood by the bathroom doors at the back, wiping her tears.

I didn't see his fist. I couldn't see it coming. A blur of movement, a subtle shift in position, and what felt like a giant rock broke my cheekbone. My head flew back and banged the wall behind me.

Fight-or-flight alarms flooded my system, with flight winning by the time I slipped out of the chair and landed on the floor under the table.

Andrea screamed. Her voice, even in peril, reminded me why I was here. Why was she here at that moment? I realized I hated doing the right thing, but I had no choice.

My face felt like someone had set burning coals in my cheek. The pain was so intense that everything went woozy for a second.

Andrea's boyfriend couldn't bend down and yank me out fast enough, so he jumped up and landed all two-hundred-twenty pounds of biker muscle on my right foot, snapping a couple of the twenty-six bones I have in there.

My scream rose higher than Andrea's—I'm embarrassed to admit it.

I have never experienced that much pain in my life. A crazy thought ran through my mind. Women experience more pain than this when giving birth. I'm sure I can handle it and still fight my opponent, even though my shorts were soiled now with urine.

I pulled my feet in under the table to avoid further damage. I wanted to turn around. I couldn't fight sitting the way I was.

Fight? How am I supposed to fight?

"Get out here!" the bully shouted.

I pushed off the wall with my good foot and slid out from under the table. I remember hearing Andrea gasp at the sight of my face.

My eye was covered in blood, and I felt part of my mouth being pulled down as the firmness of the cheek had been relaxed now that it was broken.

My hands clamped onto his ankles. I twisted his left foot out and back while doing the opposite to the right foot. It worked. The biker lost his balance and fell hard on his back.

Before he had a chance to recover, I crawled up and drove my right fist into his groin.

It was all I could think to do. He wailed and grabbed for his privates. Under any other circumstance, I would never do that in a fight, but this guy deserved it. You don't hit a woman. Ever. If you have hit a woman, then you don't have any balls. Since it felt like this guy still did, I took it upon myself to check their size with my knuckles.

The fight lasted all of ten seconds, although, to me, it felt much longer.

Where the hell were the police? I thought they were right outside.

I crawled up farther and then got a little assistance. The biker released his scrotum and grabbed my shoulders to pull me face to face.

That was a mistake.

With my left hand, I grabbed his index finger and pulled it back. My broken foot screamed, my cheek wailed in agony, and Andrea cried behind me. That was enough inspiration for me to try to rip the guy's finger right off.

He released me in a feeble attempt to get me off his finger.

My right hand dropped hard and fast, my thumb jabbing with the force of a hammerhead into his left eye.

I was about to pass out with the pain when he woke me with his terrific screams. There was something about it that made my pain decrease. For a moment, amid the chaos, I actually felt good, my anger fueled by pain, my triumph fueled by his.

When he tried to dislodge my thumb, I renewed my assault on his finger.

His finger bone snapped in my hand—another triumphant moment. I was really getting into this. It felt great, like a rush. Who knew fighting could be so rewarding?

Then, something pricked my side.

I looked down and saw two small darts sticking out of my T-shirt. They had wires connected to them.

Andrea screamed the word, *No*.

Then I felt like I'd been plugged into a Christmas tree as the cops tased me. I looked like I was choking on my tongue because (Andrea told me after) my eyes rolled back in my head, and my broken cheek gave my face an eerie countenance. Even the cops were startled when they saw me turn toward them as they pushed the button.

The volts left my system almost as fast as they entered it, but that didn't matter as I was face down on the floor of the coffee shop, unable to move.

The cops handcuffed the biker as everyone in the coffee

shop told them what had happened.

I woke in the hospital that night with a cast on my foot and crazy bandages all over my face.

Andrea sat by my bed. She explained that her ex-boyfriend had been charged with so many new offenses that bail was denied this time.

She cried when she told me how sorry she was.

I believed her.

Andrea and I moved in together a few weeks after the coffee shop incident. She talked about being on the other side when she died. Also, what it felt like to be dead. I told her I thought I'd die that day in the coffee shop.

She talked about seeing me in there, even though it hadn't happened yet.

There was something else she wasn't saying. Some secret she was keeping. I could tell by the words she chose—the things she said.

It wasn't until the morning sickness two years later that I finally got to hear the last secret from the other side, the small surprise that she saw coming into her womb.

My Stranger

The bed covers are askew, my face buried, my breath restricted. A cool sheen of sweat is on my brow, and my heart is beating against the inside of my chest.

What's happening to me?

In the dim light coming through the curtains of my bedroom window, I can see a man I don't recognize.

This had happened before, but there was something different this time. When I woke up with strangers in the past, there was always a small characteristic about the person I could remember. Something unique to them that would allow me to know who they were. Like a goatee, the style of their haircut, or the general shape or build of the person.

The man beside me was unrecognizable. He was clean-shaven and bald. No one was in the house when I went to bed last night alone. My husband has been away for five weeks on a book tour. I expected him back last night or early this morning, but my husband has hair on his head—the guy beside me does not.

I edged off the bed, doing my best not to wake the stranger. I slipped into my walk-in closet and got dressed. If I was wrong and this was my husband, I decided not to call the police. Instead, I would go through the photo albums in the cabinet downstairs and retrieve a picture of our wedding day.

My collection of photos is rare in nature. I have every page numbered, and every picture has a caption with the date. The time the picture was taken and the people's names were there, too. This helps me to recognize people based on events in my life. It would be impossible otherwise because of my condition.

In under a minute, I'm downstairs in front of the wooden cabinet that holds the photo albums.

Something thumped upstairs. It startled me enough to make me jump.

The man has wakened.

This man may not be my husband. But then maybe he is. I just don't know yet.

What would I do if he wasn't my husband? How would I ever explain that? I have a decent memory, so I know I didn't invite anyone over last night—something I would never actually do.

So, rationally, I know it had to be my man, but my husband isn't bald. He wouldn't have shaved his head without telling me first, and I needed a photo to confirm that.

My hand fumbled and slipped off the latch on the cabinet. I was shaking but managed to get a firm grasp on the tiny brass knob. I yanked open the cabinet drawer and reached in for the photo album.

The drawer was empty.

Not a single photo album or picture. I checked the other drawers and found nothing.

My husband would never move them. He knows how important they are to me.

"Hey!" the man yelled down.

I jumped. I heard him on the stairs. It sounded like he was taking them two at a time.

I was on my feet and running without thought or hesitation. I ran through the kitchen and out the back door, then launched off the back deck in seconds flat. Our small property makes it easy to get to the edge of the yard fast. I hurried around the neighbor's fence, removing me from view of the house. I had passed at least five homes before turning around to see if I was being pursued.

The street behind me was empty.

I reached for my cell phone, realizing I hadn't grabbed it in that second. There's a coffee shop about four blocks away. I would have a coffee and calm down. Then, I'd use a payphone to call my husband's cell.

Everything would work itself out, I said to myself repeatedly, each time losing more certainty.

***

The coffee shop wasn't too busy. I ordered a coffee and found a small table by the door, where I sat. Both hands cradled the cup for warmth. I spied a payphone in the corner.

The coffee shop door jingled as it opened. A familiar man stepped in and turned toward me. His eyeglasses were unique. They were rectangular with rounded corners.

The important thing for me was that I recognized something. Although, until I heard a name, I had no idea who he was.

He walked over to my table and sat down across from me. I bristled at the interruption.

The first thing he said startled me.

"I'm your husband, but you haven't met me yet today."

My mouth hung open. Not because of the introduction. That's usually how Alex does it, so I know it's him. I was shocked because if this was my husband, then who was the man I was in bed with last night? That bald man was still in my house.

I stared at his face a moment more. Do I tell him about the man at our house? What if he's stealing everything out of the house as we speak? But then, how do I explain it away? Maybe if we leave the coffee shop together and go home, Alex can confront the stranger if he's still there.

"When did you get back from the book tour?" I paused, then added, "And how did you know I'd be here?"

"Got back a couple of hours ago, and I didn't know you'd be here. I was pulling into the alley by our house and saw you running down the block. I followed you here. Is everything all right?"

Do I tell him or not? My stomach dropped. If I was going to trust anybody, it should be my husband. But what if this guy wasn't my husband?

Being face blind is a terrible thing to live with. People

don't understand it. What I suffer from is called Prosopagnosia, which basically means I can't remember faces. My memory is pretty decent, but for faces, I have to fixate on one characteristic and memorize it or try to. It can be so daunting.

"Everything's fine," I say, my voice weak. "I only wanted a coffee and thought I'd come here." My reasoning was weak; my posture, everything.

"We're almost late. Let's get that bank transfer done. Then we can head home. I'm tired from all the traveling."

His voice was different. Sometimes, I can use a voice to determine who I'm talking to. People really hate it when you talk to them for ten minutes and then call them by someone else's name.

"The bank's across the parking lot," he said. "You ready?"

"What transfer are you talking about?" I felt lost and out of sorts, so I decided to stall him because something wasn't right, and I couldn't put my finger on it. "I don't remember talking to you about any transfer."

"How could you forget?" He looked flustered. "The advance on the new novel and the royalty cheques were deposited into our new account. We need to transfer the money into our joint account for the mortgage."

Why couldn't I remember any of this? "Then why do you need me?"

"Because, honey, it's a lot of money. I didn't want to walk into the bank and do that kind of transfer without you in case they needed your signature. Now, let's get this done. I'm tired."

I remained seated. "You're being short with me. I'm not sure why."

"If I'm being short, it's because I'm tired. If I seem in a hurry, it's because I am. Now, let's go."

I checked his hair, his jacket, and his shoes. As far as I could remember, he may well be my husband. Only his voice was off. At least those were better odds than the bald guy I was in bed with not twenty minutes ago.

I dropped my half-empty cup in the garbage and followed him outside. We walked silently toward the bank until I asked, "Did you pick up a cold when you were away?"

"Over the last few days, I came down with something. It affected my voice some. Why do you ask?"

"It just seemed like your voice was different."

We entered the bank. Alex told me to wait in a chair while he lined up. I watched him from where I sat and mentally went over everything. I still hadn't forgotten the man in my home. Why were the photo albums missing, though? I may be face-blind, but I'm not stupid—I wouldn't cheat on my husband. Since I knew I would never cheat, then who was the man in bed with me this morning? And why do I have no recollection of any talk about transferring money? However, I remember the new bank account and the royalty cheques but nothing about transfers.

Alex got to the teller. He spoke to the woman momentarily, pulled out his wallet, and waited. The teller said something to him. He glanced over at me, then beckoned for me to join him.

When I got to the counter, the teller asked for my signature because of the joint account status. I signed where I was supposed to and waited beside my husband.

When we first started dating, I asked the same questions repeatedly. I needed to get settled with him to be comfortable. He understood it then, and he'll understand it now.

"Alex, what city did we get married in?"

"What?" He stared sidelong at me. "We got married in Rome, Italy."

He was right.

"Our anniversary date is when?"

The teller handed him back his access card. She gave me a weird look.

"August 14, 2004. Now, can we continue this outside?"

He walked past me after thanking the teller. I smiled and waved at the woman. She averted her eyes.

I decided to ask a different kind of question.

"Alex, have I ever miscarried?"

"What? Come on, Mary, what kind of question is that?"

"A simple yes or no. Have I ever miscarried?"

His face scrunched into a scowl. Now I was afraid again. Outside the bank, I grabbed his arm and spun him around.

"Answer me!"

He stared into my eyes a moment and said, "Yes."

He was wrong. He was guessing. I can't have babies. I can't get pregnant. Only my husband knows this.

I backed away, my hands shaking. My breath was stunted, almost like I was panting.

"Who … who are you? What have you done?"

A car pulled up, and the driver blew the horn. The guy who impersonated my husband ran to it and jumped in. They were gone before I could even think about reading the plate number.

I didn't know what to do next.

Maybe the bald guy in my house was my husband, but that couldn't be.

I ran back into the bank and told them that I had just been robbed. They called the police. When the authorities arrived, I informed them of my face blindness condition.

The cop said that was why they probably used me, so I could never identify them.

The bank manager got me a phone and set me up in a little cubicle so I could call home. A man answered. I recognized his voice immediately.

"Honey, you're home," I shouted into the phone, half lifting out of the chair they'd provided me.

"Mary, I've been home since two in the morning. Do you have your cell phone? I couldn't reach you. And why did you take off running like that this morning?"

It was all coming together. I eased back down into the chair.

"When I woke up beside you, you had no hair. What happened to your hair?"

"You don't remember the deal I had with my brother?"

His brother was out on bail. His court date was this week sometime. Alex was worried his brother was going to skip bail. He always talked about not being able to do the time.

"Refresh my memory."

"I thought my brother wouldn't have to go to jail, and he thought he would, so we made a bet. If he got convicted, I told him I'd shave my head to show support."

A thought surfaced from the deepest regions of my consciousness, nagging at me to listen to it. I was missing something.

"What happened to our photo albums in the cabinet?"

"I took them out when I got home last night so I could put a new shot of my shaved head in there for you. I must have left them on the kitchen table."

A police officer motioned to me.

"Look, Alex. Something happened at the bank today. I don't know how to tell you this, so I'll come right out and say it …" The cop stepped into the cubicle. I kept my voice low. "Honey, I'm gonna finish here, and then I'll be right home. What I have to say will be better in person."

I replaced the receiver and stood. The cop looked at his notepad, read something, and then glanced back at me.

"It looks like we've recovered your money. Since it was a transfer to another account, they just reversed it. All your money is back in your account."

I felt so relieved I had to sit. The officer continued.

"The man who did this planned on withdrawing the money by driving to another branch and taking it out. They tried to stop him at the John Street branch, but we were too late."

"Do you have any idea who it was?"

The cop looked at his notepad again. "The name on the account is Norm Macey. That name mean anything to you?"

My stomach dropped again. I lowered my head. That's why he had been familiar. That's why I recognized the rectangular glasses. And his voice was almost the same as my husband's voice. And now I know why he tried to rob his own brother. He tried to take our money to finance a run from the law. It also made sense that he knew how Alex talks to me to remind me it's him daily. Alex always says, "I'm your husband, but you haven't met me yet today."

I glance back at the police officer. "Norm is my husband's brother."

***

Afterword

This story came together because I was fascinated with prosopagnosia (face blindness). I once heard someone say this line, "I'm your husband, but you haven't met me yet today," and it inspired me to write a crime where the victim might be needed to identify someone but couldn't due to their condition. Luckily for Mary, the authorities caught onto Norm quickly, and she wasn't required to recall his facial features.

I'm fascinated by face blindness because I suffer from a lesser-known issue known as name blindness. When I meet someone and hear their name, I immediately forget it. Two names? Forget it. More than two? Never.

So, to recall a name, if I'm in a situation where it's required of me, I do something called "name association." I have to go out of my way to associate their name with something else I know or remember, attach it to that, and then recall it each time I need to use it. This doesn't happen for people once I've gotten to know them, which is a blessing.

Lastly, name blindness affects the stories I write. I've

already forgotten most of the characters' names within two chapters. I have to make a list beside me while writing to keep up. This is one of the reasons why I use real-life people —my readers—as characters in my novels because I often know their names by heart.

The Visitation

"HOW IS SHE?" JAKE asked.

The nurse cleared her throat. It sounded tinny over the phone.

"She's still in the coma. I'm sorry, Jake. It's unfortunate the chemotherapy didn't do a better job."

Jake wiped a tear from his cheek. "We knew this was coming. It's just that she had made it so far that I thought she could hold on for the wedding. It was the single most important thing for her to look forward to in the end."

"That's all she talked about last week before her relapse."

"Thanks for everything, Mary, but it's already ten o'clock, and we have to get up early for the wedding tomorrow. I gotta go. Kiss her for me."

"Try not to worry about your mother. She's in good hands here. You know she wouldn't want it any other way.

Enjoy your big day tomorrow. That would mean a lot to her."

He shook his head at the unfairness of it all. "There's no way she could ever make it in her condition, but yet, her last wish was to be there. It's so hard to bear. We were so close."

Mary cleared her throat again. "Just remember that your mother is with you in her heart. She loved Jessica and is so happy for the both of you. So, get some sleep and get through your wedding tomorrow."

Jake hung up and stared at the wall. His best man was in the other room hollering something about more drinks. His future wife was with her group, prepping for tomorrow. Everything was as it should be.

But his mother was dying, and she wouldn't be joining them, and there was nothing he could do about it.

Mary, their private nurse, was hired six months ago and, in that short time, became a big part of their family.

He decided he had time for one more cigarette before going to bed. His commitment-to-quit deadline was looming. Their marriage to each other tomorrow was his promise to Jessica that he'd never smoke again.

Outside on the back deck, he lounged on an over-stuffed cushion and smoked, gazing up at the stars, wondering why his mother was being taken from him just a few months too early. He remembered how she talked about the payoff of motherhood. She was always saying that watching her children raise their own kids was what it was all about— grandchildren. It was his mother's wish to be a grandmother, and now she would never get to see the wedding, let alone any grandkids.

The prognosis was she'd probably pass in a few days. He

should be by her side, but the wedding had been planned for over a year, with people flying in from all over the country. His mother had told him last week before she fell into the coma, that she would die a sad old woman if he didn't continue with his wedding plans.

Another payoff for her was watching her babies get married.

She always said she'd be at their wedding—swore it, in fact.

Unfortunately, that was one promise she wouldn't be able to keep. It was out of her control now.

This time, Jake couldn't stop the tears as they eased down his cheek or the torrent that followed them.

***

The groomsmen arrived at the church on time. Jake was reassured that his soon-to-be wife, Jessica, was already there and in final preparations. The ceremony would begin shortly.

His stomach twitched as he looked around at the guests seated among the pews. Everyone had come to celebrate Jake and Jessica's wedding day. They had traveled in cars, taxis, and on public transportation, taking the air they breathed for granted. They all enjoyed liberties that his mother couldn't anymore. The smiles—in some cases fake happiness—he got from them meant nothing. Sure, they were known to the family and thus invited, but they were superficial. Every one of them was here for show and maybe free food.

It was his mother who he wished was there. If everyone would leave to be replaced by his mother, only then could he really be happy.

"Jake," Mike said, slapping him on the back.

Jake jumped at least a foot off the church floor.

"Mike, you scared the shit out of me," he muttered under his breath.

Mike leaned back and looked him up and down. "I scared you? The man who was the best football player our high school ever had? The guy who broke up that bar fight two years ago when no one else would, which, by the way, got you that wonderful bride of yours." He leaned in closer, a look of concern on his face. "Nerves gettin' to ya?"

"Mike, fuck that shit. My nerves are nothing. It's my mother—"

Mike nodded. "I heard. I'm sorry. I know how much she wanted to be here."

"You don't know the half of it. Look, enjoy the show. I gotta do this thing whether my mother's dying or not."

Mike said something as Jake walked away, but he didn't hear it.

Why couldn't God give his mother a small reprieve from the pain? Just a couple of days would've been enough for her to attend her only child's wedding ceremony.

Jake strode to the back to meet with the man who would perform the ceremony. He checked on the rings and ensured everyone was signing the wedding book—he wanted a permanent record of all the posers who had shown up to witness the show.

His preference was a small wedding, something intimate and quiet. They could've had the ceremony at home, in the room next door to his mother's. But no, it had to be a church.

Jessica's family wouldn't have it any other way, and they drove his mother into the ground with their stance. So, some of the blame fell on them because they say people can hear just fine while in a coma.

Well, fuck them. They aren't dying. Fuck them all.

A loud crack of thunder shook the stone building. Darkening clouds had threatened rain for the past hour, and it sounded like they hadn't been bluffing.

After a short time, the ceremony started amid the roar outside.

Jake stood at the front of the church with his best man. The bridesmaids were dressed in pathetic pink dresses, the maid of honor standing beside an empty spot while everyone waited for Jessica's father to walk up and give her away.

It all felt so fake, so Hollywood. Real people mattered. Real love mattered. His mother mattered.

He fought to keep the tears from coming. If they did, people would confuse them for tears of joy. What they couldn't know was that the tears looming at the edge of his eyelids were more from rage at the unfairness of his missing mother than the joy of this charade.

Soft, rhythmic music started. Almost everyone got to their feet. The wedding march music reverberated off the church walls as Jessica walked to the front with her father.

Moments later, the minister read from a book in his hands as the storm's noise increased outside. Jake and Jessica performed like they'd done it before, reciting word for word without making one mistake. Only Jake's grip on his anger kept him in time, in step with every moment.

He didn't unlock his eyes from the woman he realized

had betrayed him, lured him.

Because Jessica had to have a church wedding, his mother would die alone in her bed while her only son was partying it up.

"You may kiss the bride."

That was the last thing he wanted to do, but he leaned forward as Jessica moved closer. Everyone remained silent.

The moment had come.

The second before his lips touched hers, he whispered, "You betrayed me."

Their lips touched. He felt her pause, her eyes wide and staring at him, then she kissed him. It was cold, but she kissed him.

He watched her as she glared at him.

A crackle of thunder from outside the church walls came so suddenly that everyone jumped in a collective dance move.

Jake almost laughed at the absurdity of where and what he was doing. His new wife knew something was wrong, but she had no way of knowing what it was.

When he stepped back from her, the lights in the church flickered. People gasped and looked around furtively.

The minister, attempting to calm people, asked everyone to take their seats.

The heavens opened, rain slammed the church roof, and then the lights went out. Dim emergency lighting clicked on near the exits.

The minister, bereft of his microphone, shouted, "Everyone relax! This is temporary. Please remain calm. The best part of the day is yet to come."

The doors at the front of the church banged open hard. A man in a long black trench coat stood in the opening. What was mesmerizing about the man was his height—he had to be at least seven feet tall.

The temperature had dropped enough that a cold wind blew in when both doors stood open, touching everyone with a chill.

Jake watched the man in the doorway, and it appeared—in the dim light from outside—that the man watched Jake.

"Can we help you?" Jake asked.

The man started along the aisle without speaking.

"Did you invite this man?" Jessica whispered.

He didn't respond or turn to look at her.

Something mesmerizing about the man had captured his complete attention.

A couple of the male guests stood as the trench-coated man continued up the aisle.

Jake's best man nudged his arm. "Hey, who is this guy? Why has everything stopped?"

Jake ignored him.

"Can I help you?" the minister asked as the man stopped in front of Jake and Jessica.

The church stayed silent. The only sound was the rain, the weather.

Jessica nudged Jake's arm. Knocked from his reverie, he turned to face her, then followed her gaze to the back of the church.

Jake's mother stood with a man he didn't recognize.

"Go to her," Jessica said. "We can get through the confetti and out to the limousine after you see her."

Jake walked away as if in a daze, moving to the side alcove, an area hidden from the guests.

Maybe his anger at Jessica had been misplaced. Perhaps he'd been a tad unreasonable. His mother had made it, after all.

"Mom," he stammered. "How did you get here?"

"I had help." Her voice was stronger than he expected. "You know I wouldn't miss your wedding for the world. And what a wedding it was."

Jake's heart raced like he'd been jogging. "How're you feeling? You must be doing better to have made this trip." Her wig looked like it was a replica of her own hair.

"I wouldn't dare burden you on your big day with talk of my illness. Just enjoy the moment and take care of Jessica. She's a prize, Jake. I'm sure you'll have two wonderful children and live happily. Now, don't keep your lady waiting on my account."

Jake shook his head. "I'm amazed you could make it. I don't know how you did it—I talked to Mary last night, and she said you were still in a coma."

"I was, but I had help getting here." She gripped the forearm of the man beside her. Until that moment, Jake had barely registered him. Nothing about the man was familiar, except Jake thought he recognized the suit the man was wearing.

Weird. Why would I recognize clothes instead of the man?

"I should be going now," his mother said. "You take care of that lovely lady and the two children to come."

After an intense and loving hug that spoke volumes of

their shared history, his mother was led over to the side door of the church.

Jake attempted to compose himself, his heart thudding in his chest. He leaned against a pillar and slowly turned back to look at Jessica.

She wasn't there.

No one was.

Other than the man in the black trench coat, the church was empty.

"What the fuck is this?" Jake asked, pushing off the pillar and moving forward.

"An odd question for the man who facilitated your visitation."

"My visitation? What's that supposed to mean?"

Jake moved even closer to the trench-coated man.

"What did you want most today?" the man asked. "What did your mother desire beyond anything?"

"This was my wedding," Jake said without answering the stranger. "Where is everybody?"

"What do you think will happen if you fail to answer my questions?"

Four feet separated them now.

"I have no idea. But if you don't tell me what's happening, I know one of us won't be walking out of here."

"Do you feel your threats hold weight with me?"

"What's with all the questions, asshole?"

"Your mother asked for one last request. She will pay for that request for eternity. Unless, of course, you cover her debt. Are you willing to discuss that?"

Her debt? What the hell?

"What are you talking about?" Jake asked.

"Are you willing to talk about your mother's debt?"

"She didn't have any debt. Dad left her a large estate six years ago. She had enough money for a private nurse and then some. She always provided for us and will provide for me for years to come after she passes."

Thunder clapped above them. Jake looked around the darkened church and felt an icy fear creep up his back. He fought the accompanying shiver, knowing it was impossible to have removed all the guests so fast without him hearing a single thing. So then, where was Jessica? She wouldn't have just walked out of the church alone.

"You're trying to figure out what's happening here, but I wouldn't think too hard about it. There's nothing you can do other than to answer my one question. Should your mother pay her debt, or can you cover it?"

Jake nodded, and without thinking, he said, "I'll cover it."

He looked up into the eyes of the seven-foot man and listened to what his mother had done.

Then he agreed to make sure she would not suffer for eternity.

***

The church lights turned on, blinding Jake for a moment. He raised his forearm to cover his eyes.

A collective gasp came from the guests.

Jessica was at his side. Cheers roared through the church, accompanied by vigorous clapping.

Jake's heart thumped in his chest with the knowledge of what he had to do. He thought about where his mother was, and he hated every single person staring at him. A vile, disgusting hatred enveloped him, making him want to slaughter every single soul in the building. The thought of blood covering the inside of the church made him smile wide.

The married couple ran through the throng of well-wishers to the limousine while rice and confetti were tossed on their heads.

Once inside, Jessica asked, "How did she pull it off?"

The limousine started toward the hotel, where they would prepare for that evening's dinner and reception.

Jake feigned confusion. "I have no idea, but whatever happened was a blessing. We both know how much it meant to her." To complete the show for Jessica, he reached into his inner breast pocket and pulled out his cell phone. "I will call Mary to get the latest prognosis and thank her for making it happen."

After dialing and reaching Mary, he asked her how it was possible. Jake hit the speaker button and angled the phone so Jessica could listen in, too.

"How was what possible?" Mary asked. She sounded subdued, wounded.

"My mother. Last night, she was in a coma, and today, she's all dressed up and at my wedding."

Mary gasped, then cleared her throat.

Jake glanced at Jessica, then asked, "Are you okay, Mary?"

"I'm sorry. I'm so, so sorry. Jake, your mother passed

away at two o'clock this morning. There is no way she could've been at your wedding. I'm unsure what you're saying because if you saw someone there, they were an imposter."

Jake acted as stunned as he should have felt. Jessica's eyes had widened to saucers.

"That's impossible," Jake stammered. "Jessica saw her, too. She was there, I tell you. She was there, Mary."

"I'm sorry, Jake. Your mother never left this building."

"Are you sure?" he asked.

"I'm as serious as the cancer that took her from us."

Jake hung up and wept. After a few moments, Jessica wept with him because she'd witnessed the miracle alongside him.

***

Two years later …

Jake placed the photo album back into the plastic container. Jessica had recently come home from the hospital. Their second child would follow her home in a few days.

They had two children, just as his mother said they would.

The photo album Jake had been looking through confirmed the identity of the man who had accompanied his mother on their wedding day. Jake's father had died not long after Jake was born. When going through his mother's belongings, he'd come across the photo albums and saw a picture of his father holding him. That was why he'd recognized the suit. His father had been wearing the same suit at the wedding that he'd worn in that picture thirty-eight years before.

Jessica called him from downstairs. She was still recovering from her cesarian. The staples in her stomach had just been removed twenty-four hours before.

Jake got up and went to the attic stairs. He silently prayed and descended the stairs, knowing he was doing the right thing.

Jessica called him again. She was stuck in their bedroom. Unless she wanted to piss the bed, she had to wait for Jake to take her to the bathroom.

He made his way to the kitchen. There, he grabbed a long blade, one used numerous times to slice vegetables.

He touched the sharp edge. It would work just fine.

Then he headed for their bedroom. Jessica screamed his name again. But he paid her no attention as his mother's debt consumed his thoughts.

That his mother would sacrifice eternity for him was unfathomable. That she would pay such a debt to be at his wedding, to partake in his momentous event, was enough for any man to comply with her wishes.

He couldn't allow his mother to burn for eternity.

Jessica wouldn't even perform an intimate ceremony near his mother's deathbed. Would she love him enough to do what his mother did for him?

Never.

She was the reason his mother had had to make the choice she did.

Women like Jessica were the reason for all the wrong

decisions made in the name of love.

Jake had made the right decision, though. Have the two kids, as his mother had said they would pay the debt. His kids would grow up knowing that their mother was a whore, that she had run away and moved into a whorehouse somewhere. He had tried to stop her, but she couldn't see what love was. Jessica was incapable of seeing what real love was.

What Jake was about to do was defined as real love.

Nothing was equal to the love of one's mother.

He entered the bedroom and turned off the light.

"Jake, what are you doing?" Jessica asked. "I've been calling you for over ten minutes. I really need the bathroom. Turn the light back on, and come help me up."

Jake moved forward by memory, the knife in front of him.

"Jake?" Jessica's voice took on the edge of fear. "What are you doing? I can hear you moving around. Don't make me jump. You know how much that'll hurt. Jake?"

He made it to the edge of the bed.

He placed his hand on her hip.

"Jake, watch it. You almost touched my wound."

He judged where her face would be. He touched her shoulder.

"I'm sorry, Mother. I wish I had done this sooner."

He swung the blade at Jessica's throat, his knife hand jabbing dozens of times, his mind blocking her screams.

***

Jessica screamed. She scrambled to the side and flicked

on the lamp beside the bed.

The light exposed what had become of her husband and who stood over him in her bedroom.

The enormously tall man from her wedding had returned. He stood in his long trench coat, staring down at Jake, who seemed to be having a seizure on their bedroom floor. Blood squirted out of his neck where the knife had entered.

Jessica screamed as she edged away from the stranger.

When he spoke, his voice quieted her.

"Your mother's debt has been paid. Thank you, Jake, for showing me a greater evil." The man averted his gaze to take in Jessica. "I won't be bothering you again. This was between myself, Jake, and his mother." He smiled, showing horrid red teeth. "Jake was a good sport."

The man in the trench coat glided to the bedroom door, then turned back.

Jessica panted like a dog while wondering if she was having a heart attack.

"Maybe we'll meet again one day." He shrugged. "Or, perhaps not."

Jessica didn't stop screaming until the police arrived and broke down her door an hour later.

The Chute

Earth races toward me at a rate of two hundred kilometers per hour. It's my first solo jump, or what some veterans call a static line.

The adrenaline rush courses through my sixty-year-old veins and makes my stomach weak. I know my legs and arms are shaking because of it and not just the intense wind at this speed. A firm tug tells me my main chute is opening. I looked down and tried to locate the drop zone.

That's where the difficulty starts.

The straps cause a pain in my chest. My daughter's voice is in my earphones. She's the ground coach today, guiding the jumpers to safety. She's also helping me celebrate my sixtieth birthday by skydiving at the school where she's an instructor.

But how come I'm still falling so fast? Why did they

tighten the straps so much? My speed is not decreasing.

Where's my steering toggles?

I'm supposed to guide myself to the drop zone with those things.

I glance up and immediately understand why I'm still falling so fast. My chute is tangled.

Panic causes a toxic mix in my stomach. My face feels flushed as the air slaps my cheeks back. My eyes bulge, and my body strenuously protests this abuse. I ask out loud what I'm supposed to do. I've just finished five hours of lessons, and I've forgotten everything. My daughter screams in my ear now, her words unintelligible.

The patchwork of farmland below has a life of its own as it races toward me. I decipher some of her words. Reserve chute came through in my daughter's desperate voice.

I grip a dangling line and pull.

Nothing happens.

I look down.

There isn't much time left. My left hand feels something loose near my chest. I grip it and yank.

Another firm tug from behind me, and I feel the violence of the air on my face decrease rapidly. I can't be a hundred feet from the ground. I can't see the drop zone or the skydiving building anymore. I tried to scan the area, but the trees cut off my view.

How do I land again? Do I lock my knees and ankles, or do I flare something? Trees and branches hit me.

Something hard smacks into me, knocking consciousness from my awareness.

***

Sometime later, I stand and unclip the harness, letting it fall to my feet. They taught us how to fold and pack our equipment after the jump, but I'm leaving it right where it is. While I try to locate the skydiving building, I'm not lugging that thing with me. They can come back and get it.

How long have I been out? It's dark now—the sun has dipped below the horizon. Why did no one come to get me? I touch my head and feel around for injuries. My hands come up empty—no injuries.

When I turn around, I nearly jump out of my skin. A woman of about thirty years of age is standing behind a tree, watching me.

"Are you lost?" I ask her.

She turns to go without saying a word. I yell for her to wait, but she disappears among the trees.

I try to get my bearings. I can't see the North Star. I start to walk anyway, but the same woman stops me from a few moments ago.

This time, she's standing out in the open. I wait for her to say something. After a few moments, I blink, and she's gone. Who is this woman? Why won't she talk? And why does she just watch me and then leave?

I put one foot in front of the other and enter a clearing. Halfway across the field, I know I'm going the right way. I can even see my car in the parking lot of the skydiving building. I look back toward the trees and see that crazy, mystery woman. My feet falter, and I stop where I am. Something must be wrong with her, but this time, it'll be me who looks away. I'm going to be the one who disappears.

I turn around and quicken my approach to the base.

In a matter of moments, I reached the classroom door but stopped to watch a car barrel the parking lot. The car's tires screech as the driver applies the brakes too hard. The door opens as soon as the engine stops, and a woman gets out. I watch as she stands by her open door and scans the immediate grounds. Then her eyes find me, and she stares.

I now have another woman, whom I don't know, staring at me and saying nothing. I look down at how I'm dressed. I touch my face, looking for deformations. Maybe I'm covered in blood and don't know it. Maybe I have a case of skydiving bends. I've heard that scuba divers can't come to the surface too fast lest they get a case of the bends. Maybe I fell too quickly from the sky.

I look away and open the door to where I took my classes earlier. Ah, Alexia, my daughter is here. She's crying. I thought I heard that on the headphones during my jump, but I'm puzzled about the cause of her tears.

"Is everything all right?" I ask as I make my way to her side.

Nobody responds to me. I kneel in front of Alexia and ask her what's wrong. I try to take her hand, but the sound of the main door stops me as it bangs open. It's Owen, the man who taught our skydiving class earlier today.

"We found the chute," Owen says. "He went down in a clump of trees about two hundred yards from here." He pauses as he looks at my daughter. "I'm sorry, Alexia. Truly, I am."

He's sorry? For what? What's going on?

As I stared at Owen, confused by what he was talking about, the woman from the car stepped in behind him. She takes in the whole room until her gaze stops on Alexia. Then, her face turns a heavier shade of red.

The loopy woman from the woods steps in behind the car driver woman and whispers something into her ear.

"You," the woman from the car says, pointing at Alexia. "Are in a lot of trouble."

Owen steps up to the woman to block her entrance. "Who are you? What the hell is this?"

"Do you hear that?" the woman asks.

"Hear what?" Owen says.

"Listen."

Owen appears to be listening.

"A siren?" Owen asks.

The woman nods. "Just wait till they get here. I'll explain my beef then."

The crazy woman is staring at me again. I have no idea why the police are coming. I just want to talk to and console my daughter.

"Can we help you?" I ask.

Both women stare at me. The driver says, "Not yet. It'll all be clear in a moment. I witnessed your jump from the highway. I thought I'd drop by to clear up this mess."

"Who are you talking to?" Owen asks the woman.

"Mike, Alexia's father."

"Okay, that's just rude. Get out."

Owen turns his back toward me and tries to coerce the visitor to leave. Alexia stands and tells Owen to wait.

"Who are you," Alexia asks. "And how could you

possibly be talking to my father?"

I looked to Alexia's right and saw the strange woman hidden quietly among the trees. She's moved inside the building, walked across the floor without me seeing her do it, and is staring at me.

"My name is Kramer Kay, and I'm a psychic."

The police sirens are closer.

"I'm sorry," Kramer continues. "Your father has died, but I can see him. I'm staring at him right now."

"I demand to know what's going on," Alexia shouts, wiping her eyes. Fear has gripped her voice.

I'm feeling it, too. I had no idea I was dead. This is ridiculous.

"There's a woman here—her name's Joanne Stinson. She was killed a month ago during her first jump. At least that's what I'm being told."

Both Owen and Alexia appear stunned.

Police cars pull up out front. Doors slam shut.

"Okay, maybe you should step outside," Owen says.

"No way. I'm not taking my eyes off Alexia," Kramer says. "Try me. Just try to remove me."

Feet slap the pavement outside. The door flies open, and two policemen step in past Kramer.

"She's right over there," Kramer says, pointing at Alexia.

The two officers run over to Alexia and grab hold of each arm.

"Ma'am, you're going to have to come with us."

"Why?" Alexia squirms in their grasp. "Am I under arrest? And if so, on what charge?"

"Charges are pending until we receive a full statement

from Kramer and we examine the equipment. Unless you want to offer a confession before—"

"Get your hands off me," Alexia demands.

"Ma'am, resisting arrest comes with other charges."

Kramer steps forward. "Alexia, it's because of Joanne Stinson and your father. You folded their chutes, didn't you?"

Alexia looks at Owen. I look at Owen. I can't believe what I'm hearing. So far, no one but the psychic has looked at me. Am I really dead? Did my own daughter murder me?

Kramer continued. "Joanne found out about your plan to kill your father. Was it insurance money? Is that why you did it? You folded the chutes so they'd tangle, isn't that right? You made the reserve chute useless." Kramer shakes her head. "If it was for money, you may be rich now, but a lot of good that'll do you in prison. I can prove what you did because I can talk to the dead. Joanne is here, and she's telling me everything. The authorities will need evidence, and I'll be able to offer it."

"Bullshit." Alexia spits on the floor. "I would never kill my father. I made sure those chutes were perfect. No way did I meddle with them. I'm no murderer. I'll sue you for this."

"Go ahead. I'm insured."

I can't believe what I'm hearing. My own daughter wanted me dead. But every part of my being feels Alexia is telling the truth.

"Kramer," I say, hoping she can hear me. The two officers are leading my daughter away now. "Can you hear me?"

She looks my way and nods.

"I don't feel Alexia did this. I know my daughter. She's

not capable of murder. She can barely step on an ant."

"I know. This is the only way. Let me handle it."

The cops step outside, Alexia between them. This leaves only Kramer and Owen in the building now.

I watch as Owen steps behind his desk and plops down in his chair.

"This has been a horrible day. First, Alexia's dad dies in the jump, our second at the chute school, and then his daughter gets arrested for double homicide. I feel like I'm in a state of shock."

Kramer steps closer to his desk. "I know this may be a lot to handle. I just wish we'd been here sooner. Then, maybe, we could've saved Mike."

Owen grabs a pencil off his desk and starts tapping it on the paper calendar he has spread across the surface. "Are you really psychic?"

Kramer nods.

"Then you can see dead people?"

She nods again.

"And they can tell you secrets. Like what happened to them and how it happened, and the police take that as gospel."

"Where are you going with this?"

"Come on," he gets to his feet. "I'll take you out to the plane and show you the other chutes. Take one home with you. I'll sign it out. Hand that to the police and show them how Alexia set it all up."

Owen walks over to the large board on the wall and writes the name Kramer.

"The plane has chutes six and seven. I'll sign out lucky

seven to you. Come over and sign here, and I'll help you load it into your trunk."

Kramer takes the pencil out of Owen's hand. She signs the board and follows him to the door.

I hurry to follow them. Instantly, I'm there, right behind them.

"Kramer, can Owen hear me?"

She looks sideways at me and shakes her head.

"Okay, something's wrong. He's angry. I think Owen means to hurt you in that plane."

She raises a hand and tries to brush me off.

There's nothing more I can do. Even if I want to step in, how could I?

They reach the plane and enter the fuselage through the open side door. Owen reaches out to lend a hand to Kramer. The inside is dark, but I can see just fine.

"It's over here," Owen says. "Step in a little farther."

Someone else is here. I panic and shout for Kramer to look out. Before Kramer has a chance to respond to my warning, Owen has spun around and sucker punched Kramer. She launches off her feet and hits the floor of the plane hard.

"Should've minded your own business, bitch."

Owen steps forward and flips switches in the cockpit. Lights turn on in the area where Kramer is on the floor. The engines sputter and start up. He steps back to address Kramer.

"I did it for Alexia. Joanne said she'd tell her we slept together. Joanne told me she would ruin me. She went to Alexia's dad and started blabbing, but he didn't believe her." Owen steps over and slams the plane's door shut, then continues. "I had to make sure that Joanne had an accident after that. It bothered Alexia's dad, but he let it go. Although, he still wouldn't let Alexia date me. He became a major hurdle, the last one between me and Alexia. Offing him was a piece of cake. It was my idea to celebrate his birthday here. It was all so easy, and now you're going to jump with chute number seven, and no one will ever be able to prove shit." He leans down and brushes Kramer's hair out of her face. "Once you're dead, the police will have nothing to hold Alexia on. We'll be home free. It's over, bitch, it's over."

The other people in the plane, the ones I felt earlier, step out of the shadows. It's the two officers who escorted Alexia outside not fifteen minutes ago. I watch all this in stunned silence.

"Owen Henkin, you're under arrest for the murder of Joanne Stinson and Mike Hortenson. We've recorded your full confession."

Owen appears to be shocked. He turns to run but then thinks better of it, as the only door out of the plane is right beside one of the officers, who now has his gun drawn.

"Get down on the floor and place your hands on your head."

Owen complies. He's cuffed and taken outside in under a minute. My daughter steps out of the shadows and walks to the cockpit, where she turns off the plane. Kramer sits up, her back against the fuselage wall, rubbing her cheek.

"Why?" Alexia asks Kramer. "Why did my dad still die? I exchanged his chute before the plane took off. I gave him mine. His was supposed to work. It was supposed to work."

She breaks down in tears.

"I'm sorry," Kramer offers. "Your dad's chute was fine. There was nothing wrong with his chute at all. The crazy thing is he had a heart attack almost immediately after leaving the plane. He lost his ability to function properly and died before he hit the ground. In this case, it actually had nothing to do with Owen."

Alexia looks up, her eyes awash with tears. "When the police approached me and said that Joanne had been in touch with you and that they felt Owen had killed her, I couldn't believe it at first. You helped set this trap for Owen. You all did a great job. Seeing my father killed wasn't supposed to be a part of it."

"I know, and I'm sorry. He's here. He heard everything. He even tried to warn me about Owen. Your father is a good man. I'm so sorry for your loss."

Alexia looks up, her eyes focusing on the area slightly to his right. "Goodbye, Daddy. I'm sorry."

Averting Calamity

Onalee watched as a cop followed three youths along the sidewalk. Onalee remained by her car, keys dangling in her hand, waiting, watching. It was nearing nine p.m. She should be making the trip home.

Yet, something about the officer made her stand and watch.

Simultaneously, two images entered her conscientiousness. The first one told her why the cop and the teenagers were important to each other. The second image showed tomorrow morning's newspaper headlines if she didn't intervene.

She gasped when the second image shot into her mind, her hands coming together over her chest. Sometimes, the shock of the information she received was difficult to see inwardly.

With life, fate definitely played a large role, which couldn't be avoided for the most part, but accidents were altogether different.

She thrust the car keys into her pocket and bolted through slow-moving traffic to the other side of the street. She stepped in front of the officer within minutes, making him stop.

"Excuse me," she said, trying to catch a breath. "I need to talk to you for a quick second."

The officer angled to the side to stare over her shoulder, intent on keeping an eye on the threesome he'd been following.

"What is it?" he grumbled.

"I know about your sister."

He stopped watching the teenagers to study her face. "What did you say?"

"I know about your sister. She was given up for adoption at birth. You were told about it before your mother died a few years ago."

"Do I know you or something? How could you know that?"

"I know where she is."

He stepped back, hands on his hips. "Okay, I'll bite. Where is she?"

Onalee turned around and pointed. "You see those three teenagers you were following a few minutes ago, the two guys and the girl up on the corner by the bridge?" He was nodding when she looked back at him. "The girl is your sister. She was raised in Orillia by her adoptive parents."

"How could you know something like that?"

"Go ask her where she grew up. Tell her something about having to talk to her parents and investigate further. Trust me on this."

"Okay," he said. "I get it. You knew my mother. Otherwise, this is a prank of some kind, and I don't take too lightly to shit like that."

Onalee turned away and started toward the trio by the bridge.

"Hey, wait up," he said, coming after her, staying close at her heels.

He asked her several more questions, none of which she answered.

They got to the streetlight where the threesome had turned left. The teenagers had been out of sight for maybe a full minute now.

The cop checked a couple of store windows. He looked across the street and up on the bridge, but they had disappeared.

Onalee checked her watch.

Thirty minutes before the accident.

There was nothing left for her to do. She had to get down to the docks.

She turned and ran without an explanation. The officer yelled something behind her, but she had no time to explain.

All the boat slips were full. As the summer sun set in the distance, people brought their boats in for the night.

"Hey!" a man shouted.

Onalee glanced over at the entrance to the docks about ten feet away. It was the cop again. He was bent over, hands on his knees, trying to catch his breath.

"Why did you run away like that?" he asked, through gulps of air.

"Those teenagers we lost sight of will steal a boat in the next ten minutes. For some reason, it will capsize immediately, and you will have three fatalities on your hands, your sister included."

The officer glared at her, taking a tentative step in her direction.

"Are you for real?"

"Yes, I am for real. I know a little of what the boat looks like, but not enough to identify it. With the sun almost down, we have to act fast."

He stood three feet from her now. "You walk up to me on the street and tell me you've found my long-lost sister. You point out the three people I was following after I was acting on a tip that they shoplifted from a music store, and now you're stalling me to help them get away. Is that it? Or are they actually going to steal a boat and capsize it?"

Onalee nodded. "Capsize," was all she said. It would take too long to convince him otherwise—there wasn't time.

"Right, and I believe that. Sure I do. How about I take you downtown for the night to find out who you really are and what this is all about?"

This was an all too familiar crossroads. She had to appease him, convince him to let her keep looking for the teenagers, or their deaths would be on her head.

"Look, I'm quite aware of how this looks. But before I leave, let me hang around for ten more minutes. I have to try to find those teenagers."

"What's your name?" he said, pulling out a notepad and

pen.

After she told him, he looked up without writing it down. "Are you that psychic? The one I heard solved the disappearance of a young girl found in the drywall of her parents' house?"

"That's me." Onalee pulled out a card she had printed for the readings she did for members of the public. It had her name and home phone number on it.

The officer put his pad and pen away. "For the record, I don't believe in psychics. Yet, I have heard you're the real thing. I'll give you your ten minutes. Then get out of here."

He turned and stomped away.

That was one of the first times her notoriety had come in handy.

Ten minutes came and went. A half-hour passed with no results. It was fully dark when she got to her car. She sat there staring out the windshield at nothing. Maybe this one was fate. Something she could do nothing about. She lowered her head and wept a few tears. She cried for the three lives that would be lost.

When she got home, it was just past midnight. Her work phone had voicemail. She opened a bottle of red wine and sat down by the phone. The first message was a hang up. The second was the cop from earlier. He said he'd kept her card and used it to call her. He wanted to let her know that he'd had a change of heart.

"... *after what you said at the docks, I called a friend at the RCMP detachment near your hometown, who gave you a good reference. So, I alerted the RCMP in my area for a stolen boat with three teenagers. The marine unit located them twenty minutes after they capsized, clinging to a single life jacket. They were exhausted, trying to figure out which way the shore was in the dark. All three were pulled from the water alive.*

"There's one other thing. The girl's name was Jayne Markus. She still lives in Orillia. I just left her at the hospital. She was awake and doing fine. I found out that she was adopted when she was a baby, and she's been looking for her family for the last eight years. Through this twist of fate, she found her brother, and I found my sister. Thank you, Onalee. Thank you ..."

Onalee wiped a tear off her cheek as she raised her wine glass in a silent toast to the other side.

Another successful resolution.

A calamity averted.

***

Afterword

Onalee was a character I came up with before Sarah Roberts. She's in her mid-thirties, so she's older than Sarah, but as you'll see in a few more stories, Onalee possesses some of the same spirit Sarah has.

When Sarah Roberts was developed for her own series, I retired Onalee and Kramer Kay, two psychic characters that Sarah was based on forever.

This set of short stories is Onalee's final resting place.

The Ghostwriter

I will never forget it.

Ever.

It was the scariest day of my life, yet the most beautiful.

I never thought anyone'd completely take me. I'm a writer of autobiographies. I meet with men and women in old age homes and write their stories as they narrate them. I'm quite successful at what I do. Few people are in this line of work, so the competition is small.

I was directed to room 213, where my client was resting. His name is Markus John. He's supposedly ninety-six years old and ready for a lift to the ever after. I was so excited because I had pre-empted this client, and as far as I knew, this guy had a fantastic story about the Second World War. He was in some kind of elite group, and he wanted to discuss how it affected his family.

Usually, I get dribble from my clients. Half of them have difficulty remembering things. I've even had a few who were so lost with Alzheimer's that we couldn't go on. Sad, I know, but I try. I always try.

The blond attendant stopped in front of room 213 and waved me in with a flourish of her arm. As I entered the room, I glanced at her nametag: Rebecca.

"Thank you, Rebecca."

When I turned back to smile at her, she was gone. She was undoubtedly off to perform other duties that involved the frail, the old, and the sick. How noble.

A large man lay in the bed, covers neatly wrapped around him, stopping just short of his neck. His eyes were closed. I hesitated. Maybe this wasn't a good time. It was set up yesterday by phone. We agreed I'd come at one p.m. I'd leave by four p.m. He needed his rest. We'd just try to get as much done as possible in that time.

A table and chair were set up by the bed. I set down my laptop, booted it up, and sat in the chair. When he woke, I wanted to be ready.

"I am ready," he mumbled.

I jumped. He startled me. I didn't expect him to talk or read my mind. At least, that's how it felt. His voice was raspy, distinct. "I'm sorry, I didn't know you were awake."

"My eyes aren't open, but I'm awake," he said. "My time is short. Are you ready?"

"Yes, of course. Do you feel up to starting now?"

"I don't have much choice. I will be brief. Please pick up what you can. Then, piece it together later. You'll understand."

His voice had an octave I couldn't place. Not that I'm a music teacher. It's just that I've never heard a voice sound that way, like it was coming out of a flute with a reed for a voice box. Yeah, as if a flute was talking to me, but deeper.

His clipped sentences, his resonant voice, and the way he talked with his eyes closed made his story one I'll never forget.

This man had seen war, death, loss, and bravery. He'd been shot twice and stabbed once. He'd seen more than most in his time. More than I would ever dream of seeing or want to.

Sitting in that room that day, I realized what motivated me. This man, Markus John, humbled me. I wanted to hug him and tell him it would be okay. I only wished I had a father half the man Markus was. Actually, I wished I had a father.

My father left us when I was eight years old. I never heard from him nor saw him again. My mother forbids the use of the name *father* in our house. There could be something to why I do this job after all. Maybe a part of me is searching for the story of a decent old man, one I can hold on to and not let go.

Markus surprised me an hour into his tale. He opened his eyes. He had one glass eye and a soft blue tinge surrounding a green outline for the other. His good eye pierced me. It felt like he could look right through me with that one eye. What surprised me was my dad had a glass eye, too.

After a time, he started talking about his daughter. He said the story we were doing was for her and only her. He would explain at the end how I was to get this story to his daughter, and she would understand everything when reading it.

His goal today is forgiveness. He displayed compassion like I'd never seen. It was an honor to ghostwrite his life.

I took notes and scrolled every bit of pertinent information, and while I listened, I was taken aback by this man hour after hour. I almost got lost as he talked about his connections with an underground organization. I listened, I typed, but I wasn't there. I was in his story, lost, floating through it. His presence and the things he had done in his life took my breath away. I had been doing this professionally for over four years, and no one had ever brought humanity the level of vigor and humility that this man had.

I think what I related to the most was how he had to leave his family to fight in the war. But after the war, he could never return.

"I was part of an elite group. We infiltrated levels of government in more than one country." His eyes were closed again. He paused, coughed, then continued. "My name has been changed, my face altered. I've been moving from one country to another since the war. There's always someone after me. But that's over now. They're all dead."

It was past four p.m. I could see him tiring as he tried to finish. Around four-thirty p.m., he said he was too tired to continue.

He closed his magnificent eye and talked a little more. The last thing he said stopped me as I closed my laptop.

"What was that, Mr. John?" I asked.

"I said I died years ago."

A single tear descended his cheek. And then his breathing

was louder than his voice. I could tell he'd fallen asleep.

I gathered my things and left the room with an understanding of what he meant by his last comment. He'd died years ago by the loss of his family, the war, the loss of people he knew and loved. He'd died years ago by the inequality of life.

Sometimes, the pain we bear seems insurmountable, unfair even. I understood this man more than I wanted to. I only wished I had a daddy like Markus John.

I realized I hadn't figured it out when I left the building. He'd said this project was for his daughter and that I could get it to her after we were done.

I decided to come back tomorrow for more details.

***

When I got home, I couldn't stop thinking about Mr. John. It inspired me to open up the old photo albums my mother had left me after she died fifteen years ago. Cancer took her, bless her soul.

The photo albums were in the attic, right where I left them after my mother's funeral. I brushed off the dust and started through them. It was only eight p.m. I had a glass of wine and all night to reminisce.

I got through one book and opened the second one. On the third sleeve, I could see some pictures slid in behind others. I pulled a few out. A faded picture with a man sitting and a woman standing caught my eye. I set my wine glass down and stared.

Even though the picture was faded, I could tell it was my

mother, but the man was hard to discern. I pulled and yanked picture after picture until I found a better one.

This time, I was shocked.

Three people were in this picture: my mother, me at around seven years old, and my father, who looked remarkably like Markus John. Or rather Joseph Hardy, as we knew him then. He had a patch over the eye that would receive glass as a replacement.

I was up and out of the house in less than five minutes. I drove like a maniac and got to the retirement home in a twenty-minute flat.

Rebecca wasn't at the front counter. I approached the woman and asked to see Mr. Markus John.

"Hold a minute, ma'am. I don't recognize that name."

I checked her nametag: Samantha. "I was here this afternoon," I continued. "Mr. John dictated his autobiography to me. We agreed to meet now, at nine p.m.," I lied. My heart was racing. I found it hard to breathe. I had to get in. I needed answers.

A binder was open in front of Samantha. Her slow and nonchalant way of turning the pages was driving me crazy. *Come on*, I shouted in my head.

"It appears that there is no one here by that name."

I couldn't believe what I was hearing. She had no idea how to do her job.

"I was here earlier. Markus John related his life story to me. I'm an autobiographer. He was in room 213. Rebecca was the woman behind the counter. She showed me down the hall. Please check your books again."

Samantha cracked a smile. I was incensed by how rude

she was being.

"I'm one of the staff supervisors. We don't have a Rebecca on staff. This entire complex is one level. There is no room numbered 213. I'm afraid you must have the wrong building, ma'am."

Absolutely absurd.

No way. I wouldn't believe it. I could see the room I was escorted to earlier. It was down the hall on the left.

I turned from Samantha and strode to the door. I could hear her protesting behind me. I got to the room and looked in.

My hand went to the doorframe to steady myself. The room was a small cafeteria for the employees. No Markus John. No old man sleeping. No bed.

I looked around, ignoring Samantha. I know I'm right on this. I was only here four hours ago.

"The woman earlier, her nametag said Rebecca. Can you re-check your staff names?"

"It's not necessary. I do all the hiring. We do not have a Rebecca on staff. Now, if you please, leave the building. I don't want you upsetting our live-ins."

I walked away in a daze. This wasn't happening. It couldn't be happening. I don't take drugs. I don't hallucinate.

I stood by my car, trying to piece it all together.

I remember one thing: he said he'd died years ago. I thought he meant emotionally. Could he have been speaking *literally*?

Movement caught my eye. A man was standing by a tree about a hundred yards from me. A woman stood to his right. I squinted in the light of dusk. The man waved and turned away. The woman followed.

When he turned from me, one last ray of summer sunlight caressed his back. It was Markus John and Rebecca. There was no doubt in my mind.

Then they were gone.

I have no idea where. They were just gone like they disappeared in a wisp of air.

It took me a few weeks to get over it. I cried. I grieved. I couldn't write for a month. Not many people could meet their parents after they were gone.

But I did. I got to because my dad was amazing. He'd done it all for us according to his life and recited story.

My daddy was my hero.

It took me another month to know who Rebecca was. A search online, a family tree, and hours of labor revealed the answer.

I found an old picture of my mother from her high school days before I was born.

Rebecca was my mother's middle name. She was just as beautiful as when I met her at the retirement home.

I can't seem to stop crying.

Goodbye, Mom and Dad ...

In Passing

Onalee approached the elderly couple. Both of them stared at her.

"Hello," the woman said, her mouth forming a soft grin. It seemed to be a feeble attempt at easing the tension.

"Good afternoon, ma'am. My name is Onalee. My colleagues and I are in the area today, volunteering for the Hospital for Sick Children. We're delivering pamphlets." Onalee stopped talking as the woman raised her hand.

"I've got the eye for these things," she said. "I can tell who you are." The woman leaned closer. She angled her head slightly to the right and lowered her voice. "You're a seer. You're able to see and hear things that others can't."

This was the first time someone could identify her ability just by looking at her. For a brief moment, she felt as exposed as a fully clothed sun worshipper at a nude beach.

"How could you know something like that?"

The woman moved a step closer and held out her hand. "Please, help us. I'd like you to talk to our grandson."

"I'd love to, but I need to continue delivering—"

"It wouldn't take more than a few minutes. Please, our grandson is quite distraught." The woman pointed to the house. "This was his parents' house." She turned back to Onalee. "Our grandson is in the kitchen right now but doesn't live here anymore. He resides somewhere else, yet he refuses to leave. My husband and I thought that maybe you'd be able to talk to him. Help him see through such strong emotions."

Onalee looked across the street as the other volunteers went from house to house. "May I ask your names?"

"I'm Edna, and this is my husband, William."

Edna waved toward the door, and Onalee stepped past her. She felt obligated in moments like these, as if they were honey and she was a shy bear.

When Onalee reached the front door, she bent at the waist and peeked through the screen. The kitchen was directly ahead, just down a small hall. A young man sat at the table wearing a leather jacket and black motorcycle pants.

"May I come in?" she asked through the screen. "I'd like to have a word with you."

When no response came, she opened the door. He hadn't given permission, but Edna had.

When Onalee got to the kitchen table, she took in her surroundings. Large windows opened to the backyard. A middle-aged man and woman were working on weeds in the back garden.

"Can we talk for a few minutes?" she asked the young man.

He tapped his fingers on his leg and still offered no response. He seemed high-strung and agitated. He looked at her and then back outside at the two people weeding, specifically following the movements of the man, who Onalee now assumed was his father.

"Can you tell me your name?" Onalee paused. "Where do you live? Your grandparents out front asked me if I could come and talk to you."

His jaw tight, teeth clenched, he said, "My name is Burt. It's spelled with a U, not an E."

Onalee glanced at her watch. She needed to get back outside to the other volunteers, so this had to be quick.

She sat opposite him and asked, "Why are you so angry? Has something happened that you'd discuss with me?"

"I have business with my father. I have to clear things up. He's out back." Burt clasped his hands together on the table.

"I'm a stranger, someone you can tell anything to without reproach. Your grandparents specifically asked me to talk to you, which would be helpful before confronting your father."

Burt didn't move or say a thing. He just sat there, staring out the back window.

"Okay, if you're unwilling to talk to me, then let's bring in your parents. I told your grandparents I'd help, and don't lightly give my word."

Onalee got up and opened the back door.

When the door opened, the man stood quickly and gawked at her.

"Can I help you?" He dropped the tiny shovel in his hand

and marched toward her. "What are you doing in my house?"

Onalee moved backward into the kitchen while holding the door for Burt's parents to enter.

"I asked what you're doing here."

"Edna and William asked me to help." Onalee nodded at Burt's mother, who stepped into the kitchen, too. "I assume they're your parents?"

When the woman heard the two names, she gasped and raised a hand to cover her mouth, her eyes already watering.

"That's ridiculous," Burt's father said. "If you don't leave immediately, I'll call the police."

"Edna and William were just in the front yard. They asked me to come in and talk with your son, Burt. I am not here illegally."

Burt's father reached out to hold his wife up.

At that moment, Onalee realized her mistake. "Wait," she said. "I think I understand what's happened here. Edna and William passed away some time ago, didn't they?"

Burt's dad gazed at her with steady eyes. His wife leaned on the counter, wiping her nose with tissue. She spoke first.

"My parents died in a car accident seven years ago. How did you know them?"

"I don't know them. They asked me to come in and try to help Burt." Onalee gestured at him on the kitchen chair, still staring at his father.

The father took a step toward her. "That's impossible. Our son, Burt, died in a motorcycle accident a year ago. What kind of joke is this?"

She glanced at Burt, then back at his parents, trying to piece it together.

"Please, allow me to explain." She paused a moment to collect herself. "I'm a seer. The problem is, sometimes I can't tell if the people I talk to are on this plane or the other. I'm sorry for my rudeness and for your loss." Everyone took a breath. "However, something still has to be dealt with."

"Alive? Dead? Speaking with people on different planes?" The father appeared baffled. "As far as I can tell, this kitchen has three people—you, my wife, and myself." He glanced around. "No one else is here."

"Your son has told me his name is Burt, and it's spelled with a U, not an E. He was specific in that. He's sitting at this table right now, quite distressed. He says he wants to resolve something with his dad before he goes home."

"Home? This was his home."

"Not his real home, where we all come from." Onalee turned to the son. "Talk to me. Tell me what you want to say to your parents."

She knew how this looked. She was a strange woman who had just shown up in their kitchen, staring at an empty chair while pretending to speak to their son.

Burt turned toward her. "Tell my father that I'm sorry for taking the bike. I know he worked for years to buy his first Harley. He saved his money and waited for the day when he could buy it. I just wanted to show it to my friends. I need him to know that I'm sorry. I'm not leaving until he knows."

Onalee turned back to the parents. Burt's father was shaking his head as if struggling with the urge to throw the stranger out of his house while hoping she was actually talking to his dead son.

"Your son wants to apologize for taking the Harley. He

told me he knows how hard you saved and how long you waited to buy it. He said that he just wanted to show it to his friends. I think he's quite aware of the mistake he made."

The mother stepped back into the wall, her eyes wide.

The father's face drew inward like he was more serious now.

"Are you saying that my son is here right now?"

Burt's mother clung to her husband's sleeve. Tears made her mascara track down her cheeks.

Onalee nodded. "He's wearing black motorcycle pants and a leather jacket."

"Ask him the name of his grade five teacher. Only he'll know this because she lived next door to us."

Test questions were nothing new. They never bothered Onalee, while at the same time, they allowed the rest of the conversation to continue unimpeded by disbelief.

Burt told Onalee, and she turned back to the parents. "Mrs. Gordon," she said. "He really wants you to know that he's sorry."

"Tell him it's okay," the father said without delay. "No bike was worth his life. We're sorry, too. We love you so much, Burt."

Onalee saw Burt's agitation dissipate. He rose from his chair and walked over to his parents. He tried to touch them but couldn't.

Onalee had witnessed that before—the realization that you've passed on. Some know right away, others know in time, and still, some lost souls never really figure out that they're dead. Burt knew when he couldn't touch his father. With a tearful goodbye, he headed for the back door.

His grandparents, Edna and William, were waiting just outside for him. Edna looked at Onalee and mouthed the words, *thank you.*

Onalee turned back to Burt's parents, but they had disappeared.

She was alone, the kitchen empty.

She heard footsteps on the stairs.

A woman asked, "Is someone there?" Then she heard, "Damn ghosts."

Onalee stepped into the hallway and was confronted by an elderly woman.

"Oh," the woman said. "You startled me. What are you doing in my house?"

"I was deceived into cleansing it. I was asked to enter by the previous tenants," she said as she realized how the parents were in on it, too. They had all conspired to bring Burt home.

"The people who lived here before are dead," the elderly woman said.

"I know, but their son lived in your kitchen for the last year or so."

The woman looked over her shoulder at her husband, who had followed her down the stairs. "I knew it, what with the table always making that noise. It would rattle and thump, like someone tapping their fingers on it in agitation."

"They won't be bothering you anymore. They've all moved on."

Onalee explained to the new owners of the house what had just transpired in their kitchen.

When she was done, she rejoined her volunteers,

canvassing the neighborhood.

Saving Mikey

"Don't forget, Walter will pick you up after school so we can get an early start on our trip to Toronto." Janice blew her nose and continued talking about Walter and his doctor in Toronto.

Mikey tuned his mother out as he stared down into his bowl of alphabet soup. Why did his mom give him alphabet soup for breakfast? He hadn't had alphabet soup in years.

"Mom, why am I eating this for breakfast?"

Janice turned to look at Mikey. "For the past few minutes, I've stood here talking to you about the expected telephone call from the doctor regarding Walter's condition, and all you can ask me is why you're eating alphabet soup for breakfast. Come on, Mikey, I know you're only twelve, but you should think about other people sometimes instead of always focusing on yourself." Janice put on her best, I've-been-offended look. "If you must know, we ran out of cereal, and that can of alphabet soup has been sitting in the cupboard for I don't know how long."

Janice stepped out of the kitchen, leaving Mikey to finish breakfast alone. She shouted a reminder from the other room that Walter would pick him up after school today because they had to be in Toronto early.

Mikey and Walter never got along in all the seven years his mother had been seeing Walter. Mikey's real father had died when he was two years old, so Walter had been the closest thing to a dad—a lousy one, though.

Mikey lowered his spoon, scooped noodles in sauce, and angled it toward his mouth. He looked back into his bowl and was stunned to see the soup defy gravity by moving on its own. The letters were forming words right before his eyes.

He leaned back, staring down his nose at the soup.

The noodles came together to spell out; *dont get in the car*.

Startled, he dropped his spoon and called for his mother. She ran into the kitchen, checked the soup, and then looked at her watch.

"Breakfast is over," she said. "Along with the games. Let's go. Time for school."

Twenty minutes later, he trudged along the sidewalk, looking for stones to kick as he made his way to school while thinking about his morning soup and its cryptic message. Could it mean that he wasn't supposed to go to Toronto? Or was he just supposed to avoid being picked up by Walter?

How would he explain his absence to his mother, though? And why couldn't he walk home after school like he did every other day? Could it be because Walter was an alcoholic and had liver cancer? That didn't make sense. The man was sick, but he knew how to drive a car.

One night about two weeks ago, in a drunken stupor of her own, his mother had said that Walter drank way too much. Mikey felt that his mother drank too much, as well. That was the real reason why he got alphabet soup for breakfast today—because his mother was hungover and couldn't remember where she'd put the cereal box the last time.

He stopped at the streetlight across from his school. Did he really see words form, or was it his imagination? Could it be possible that someone or something was trying to warn him?

The light changed, and Mikey crossed the street, where he then ambled to the front doors and entered K.N. McKnight Elementary School.

His morning was uneventful, but the afternoon proved long as he ruminated on the warning. He had no reasonable excuse not to get in the car, at least nothing he could come up with because his mother wouldn't accept cryptic messages in soup bowls as a justification.

Near the end of the school day, Mikey collected his knapsack and said goodbye to his friends, then started for the parking lot. He had never had such an important decision to make in his short life.

Should he get in the car and face the consequences the warning was trying to help him avoid? Or should he walk home and face the consequences of his mother's wrath? Either way, he was destined for trouble.

Knowing his mother would be super mad at him, he waited in the usual spot for Walter for at least ten minutes before he started to wonder if Walter was even coming.

The school buses had loaded and were leaving. Students whom their parents picked up were already heading home. In a few more minutes, the school grounds would be all but deserted, but for a few students coming out late and teachers leaving the building for their cars.

Mikey glanced at the road and saw no sign of Walter, so he started walking home. He wouldn't have to worry about the prophecy of not getting into the car if there was no car to pick him up. If he'd left school when all the other students had left, he'd almost be home by now anyway.

He quickened his pace to get home fast to avoid meeting Walter on the way.

He was five blocks from home when he saw Walter's beat-up Chevy come rattling toward him.

Something was different about the way the Chevy moved. The car swerved to the right, then corrected left.

It slowed when Walter saw him, then stopped beside him.

"Get in the car," Walter ordered through the rolled-down passenger window. "Come on, let's go."

Mikey took off his knapsack and stood there staring inside at Walter, clenching the straps in his hands. As the seconds ticked by, he watched Walter sitting in the driver's seat, staring straight ahead. After a whole minute, Walter turned slowly to look at Mikey.

"Well, get in. What're ya just standing there for?"

"I'll walk. It's not too far." Mikey's stomach twisted with butterflies.

Walter opened his door and rushed around the front of the Chevy. He bent down to get close to Mikey's ear.

"You gonna get in, or what?" he whispered.

Walter's hot breath coated the nape of Mikey's neck. Those future words given to him earlier in the day were serious because he also smelled booze on Walter's breath. Alcohol, combined with the odd way Walter had driven the car while approaching Mikey, told him to walk home and not get into any car with Walter. He wouldn't change his mind now—unless Walter grabbed him.

Walter stood upright, smiled awkwardly at Mikey, and then stepped backward, to Mikey's relief.

Then he lumbered around the hood of the car again and got in the driver's side. Once settled, he leaned across the front seat and raised his head to look at Mikey.

"You're worried about my driving skills, aren't ya? I'll show you how well I drive. You just watch."

His words were cut off by the loud screeching of the rear tires as Walter slammed the gas pedal down in a feeble attempt at burning rubber. Walter jerked the steering wheel so that the Chevy would do a U-turn while smoking up the street. In seconds, Walter and his Chevy were barreling down the normally quiet street. Moments later, the car disappeared around the corner up ahead.

Shouldering his knapsack, Mikey resumed walking home, his legs rubbery with fear, even though he was grateful not to be in that car with Walter. He had been able to listen to the prophecy.

His thoughts were interrupted by a thunderous crashing sound, followed by breaking glass.

Someone screamed.

The noise was coming from the general direction of his house.

Mikey ran, hoping nothing had happened to anyone he knew, but deep down inside, something told him that it was probably Walter and his Chevy. One city block later, Mikey heard a siren in the distance. He ran faster and finally turned the corner that led to his house.

Three houses away, the Chevy was now part of the huge Elm tree on his front lawn. The passenger side was completely crumpled to the point where it looked like half a car. The Chevy's engine had caught fire and was now consuming the remainder of the vehicle.

If Mikey had gotten into that car, he would have been crushed like a tiny ant, with the fire already reaching inside the car.

Mr. Martin, their neighbor from across the street, had abandoned his lawn mower to pull Walter out of the driver's seat. Walter lay on Martin's legs near a fresh pile of grass shavings. A small crowd of neighbors formed a semi-circle a dozen meters from the car, watching the flames lick higher.

It was Mikey's mother who seemed to have lost her mind as she stood in the middle of the street, as close as she could get without getting burned, screaming Mikey's name through tears and choked sobs.

She must have thought he was inside the vehicle—or what was left of him—crushed against the tree.

The fire trucks raced around the corner behind him as Mikey started walking again.

His mother dropped to her knees when she looked his

way and saw him walking along the side of the road toward her.

Mikey smiled as he knew of a guardian angel out there whose task today had been *Saving Mikey*.

The Accident

Susan Manning wondered if things could worsen as she left the office late. She raced out of the building and headed for her car, hoping to make her lunch date with Greg. On her way across the parking lot, she looked up at the drab sky and wondered if rain was coming.

Why couldn't things just go smoother?

She paid the attendant at the small kiosk by the entrance and retrieved her car keys. In her hurry, she failed to see a slight depression in the pavement. Keys in hand, briefcase suspended under her arm, she turned into the hole, twisted her ankle, and snapped off the heel of her favorite red Italian shoes.

"Shit."

When she glanced back at the attendant, she saw that she was a source of amusement for him. After offering him a harsh stare, she turned and hobbled to her car. She set her briefcase on the hood, grabbed her other shoe, and smacked it against the pavement until its heel broke, too. Now, she had a more balanced walk.

Maneuvering out of the lot wasn't difficult, but getting her anger in check was. She squealed her tires and turned onto Shuter Street, heading toward Yonge Street. No matter how bad things were, she couldn't miss her lunch date with Greg.

A slow-moving Honda hindered her progress. It had to be going twenty kilometers per hour. Irritated already, she edged into the opposing lanes, but there wasn't a chance to pass.

A red light up ahead caused the Honda driver to slow too early.

Susan tapped the horn once. She was going to be late. The last thing she needed was for Greg to think she stood him up. That would really top off her week well.

After the light turned green, and still four blocks from her turn at Yonge Street, they were crawling along with more cars piling up behind her. She laid on her horn, exasperated now.

The vehicle ahead maintained its slow speed.

Susan couldn't see through the back window of the Honda because the dark tinted windows blocked the view. She could only sit there and wait until the Honda got out of her way. Horns blared behind her, raising her blood pressure further.

She glanced down at the clock on the dashboard and saw that she would be late to meet Greg. Her lunch break was already short enough.

As the light at Yonge and Shuter approached, she breathed a sigh of relief. Susan could get around whether the Honda went north or south because Yonge Street had a double lane.

She tapped her brake to slow for the traffic light. The Honda moved to the right, allowing Susan to skirt around it. The light turned green, and Susan shot into the intersection without letting her foot off the accelerator.

She looked over her shoulder to see the Honda continue through the intersection.

A large dump truck was coming too fast. For a brief moment, Susan understood it wasn't stopping for the red light. Before she turned away, the dump truck hit the Honda, mounted it, and approached her car.

She failed to compute that she was also in the path of the behemoth truck and its large silver grill as it bore down on her.

It hadn't lost any speed moving through the small, imported Honda.

Susan's car got hit from behind, even as she attempted an evasive move. The impact shoved the back bumper into the trunk on its way through the back seat.

In a matter of seconds, Susan's car was a complete write-off.

***

She stopped in the middle of the street beside a yellow taxi in the northbound lane.

The taxi driver's mouth hung open, his eyes wide. Susan

tried the door but found it to be jammed. She reached down to lower the window, but the switch wasn't working. Then, wondering why she hadn't noticed it, she saw that the window was no longer there. It'd been shattered in the impact with the dump truck.

Susan grabbed the door frame and jimmied herself up and out of the car.

What a mess, she thought as she surveyed the damage. Her car didn't look like it could get from A to B anymore.

She turned to look at the Honda, or what used to be a Honda. After making contact with the truck, it must have caught the curb and flipped onto its roof. The engine block and front dash area got the worst of it. She wondered if the driver of the Honda would be able to walk away from such a wreck.

Small crowds of people were beginning to mill around the accident scene. A siren could be heard off in the distance.

A man in a white shirt and tie yelled that he was a doctor and dropped down to the driver's side window of the Honda. He reached into the car and hesitated while looking at his watch, probably feeling for a pulse.

Susan looked past him to the other side of the car, where a tall brunette stood up. This woman had to be the driver of the Honda because her forehead had blood on it. It trickled down the side of her face.

Wait, why hadn't she checked herself for injuries yet? Susan quickly scanned her beige business suit and found nothing amiss. Then she reached for her face, her hands coming away clean.

The word miraculous came to mind. Escaping such a

close call was a cause to celebrate. Maybe some luck was still with her after all.

When she returned to the Honda, the brunette started walking toward her and was now standing four feet away.

"Pretty scary, huh?"

Susan's gaze moved from the Honda to the woman, then back to the Honda.

She nodded. "Yes, we're lucky to be walking away from such a close call."

Her surroundings seemed to take on a new clarity. People milled around her, the police arriving and the paramedics disembarking their ambulances to attend to the injured.

But no one came to the two women who had been the drivers of the wrecked cars. It seemed as if no one even saw them standing in the middle of the street.

"Who were you driving with?" Susan asked. "Are they hurt badly?"

Paramedics reached in through the Honda's door, trying to pull someone out.

"I was alone," the brunette whispered.

Susan frowned, then glanced at the brunette.

But the woman was gone.

Instead, an intense brightness rose beside her. Susan's arms came up to protect her face out of reflex. It was like looking at the sun, yet it didn't hurt her eyes. This light had surrounded the brunette and enveloped her, lifting her away from Susan.

Other people appeared to be greeting her within this light. It was the strangest thing Susan had ever seen. The others were transparent, and they seemed to be floating. But that couldn't be.

It took all of Susan's courage not to look away. There was something beautiful about what she witnessed, something magical, and it held her rooted to the spot.

A moment later, it was over. The brunette was gone, and the light was gone. The street beside Susan was empty, where the woman had stood less than ten seconds before.

Susan placed a hand on her chest and looked back at the Honda.

The paramedics were still pulling someone out through the window. Her heart racing at what she'd just witnessed, she edged closer for a better look. In the deepest recesses of her consciousness, she knew what was going on and what had happened.

On the concrete now, the paramedics pushed on the brunette's chest, trying hard to revive her.

Susan couldn't handle it anymore.

Just as she suspected, the brunette didn't make it, and Susan had just been talking to her ghost. She turned around and headed back toward her car.

But another crew of paramedics was already there, pulling someone out of her driver's seat. Susan stopped, her mouth open as she watched the familiar beige business suit she wore on the woman's body coming out of her car.

Something pulled on her like she was tethered to a rope. It was a small tug on her torso. Then, her mother stood beside her in a soft luminescence, her hand held out.

"I've come to take you home," her mother said.

Susan felt the words more than heard them as her mother's mouth hadn't moved.

More people materialized behind her mother. All the family members that had passed before her came into view—aunts, uncles, cousins, and many more, some barely recognizable.

Susan was moved to tears as she was guided forth.

The street, the paramedics, and the police officers roaming the accident scene disappeared as Susan made the journey home into love's embrace.

The 911 Caller

I ADJUST MY HEADSET and wipe my brow. My nerves are trying to settle back to a relative calm. After twelve years as a 911 operator, some calls still rattle me. All the training in the world can't prepare anyone for a child wailing for their mother. Lately, almost all the calls I seem to take are with people yelling as if their soul is tormented.

My supervisor idles by. I feel him stop behind me.

He makes a gesture with his head. The kind that asks the question is everything okay?

I nod in the affirmative, but he isn't looking at me.

My computer screen has lit up, the red light above my terminal. I have a call coming in. My peripheral vision tells me Marshall is moving away to tend to something else.

"You've reached 911. What's the emergency?"

There's static but nothing else. My screen has

illuminated, but caller identification hasn't come up. I have no idea who or where the call originates, which is strange.

I slap the desk hard enough to get Marshall's attention. He looked over, and I waved for him to return to my cubicle.

"What's the emergency? Is anyone there?" I ask in the calm voice I've been trained to use.

Then I hear a woman's voice. It sounds like it's coming from a tunnel with vehicular traffic racing by. I can detect a sort of hollowness combined with the periodic *whoosh* sound of cars.

"... my daughter is having a seizure ..."

Marshall is by my side. He looks at the operator to my left and right. He hits a few buttons on the keyboard in front of me, but nothing happens to the computer. He's having as much success getting my screen back up as I had.

The woman says what sounds like three words, but it's indecipherable. I ask her to repeat it.

"Be careful, Nina."

I lean back in my chair, dumbfounded.

My name is Nina.

It feels like the caller is talking directly to me. Not many people are called Nina. The moniker is out there, but it's not all that common.

Marshall turns and stares at my chair. He has what looks like a frightened expression on his face. A call for help has come in, and we can't do anything about it. A glitch in the technology has blinded us.

The calls are recorded as they come in. This will be a call I want to playback.

I yank the headset from my ears. "Did we get a fix on the

location?"

Marshall shakes his head. "The computer seems to have a mind of its own."

I have a funny feeling my supervisor is talking to the operators around me. Maybe Marshall doesn't want to meet my eyes because he is at a loss for words with the caller's reference to my name.

I should be the one who is at a loss for words. I didn't recognize the voice and had no idea how a caller could know my name. I go over numerous possibilities and come up with the most plausible explanation.

It's a random coincidence. Rare, sure, but random, too.

Maybe Nina is the name of the girl having the seizure.

Some time has passed, and after checking the clock, I realize my shift is over. A wave of butterflies cascade through my stomach. That call came in an hour ago. It would be an extremely rare occurrence for me not to take even one more call in the last hour.

Something was happening.

It was not just a random act of fate. No, something was happening to *me*.

While walking home, I watch my back. It's not every day someone tells you to be careful. I now believe that using my name was a coincidence, but I'd hate to find out that the one time I heard a prophecy, I didn't listen.

All safe and sound, lying in bed, I can't sleep. Something's still bothering me. I feel like I'm being pulled to the answer. It's a feeling unlike any other.

But an answer to what?

I fell asleep then, questions, answers, and thoughts of

danger circling in my brain.

***

The sun bore down, bouncing off the pavement, channeling through me. I feel the light, but I'm not warmed by it. I wondered if I was coming down with something.

It happened when I was two blocks from work. I watched the flow of traffic passing at the light in front of me while waiting for the light to change so I could cross. The moment the light changes and I step onto the pavement, I hear a cry for help.

I turn back to see a woman bent over a teenage girl. The woman is fumbling with her cell phone as the girl lies on the sidewalk, trembling like she is having a seizure of some sort.

I spin around to head over and offer assistance, but I fail to see the pickup truck turning into the lane I had just occupied.

Horns and screeching tires wailed in concert with my scream. A second later, I blinked, stood up, and ran to the girl on the sidewalk. The woman doesn't even look at me as she fumbles with her cell phone. After several curse words, I hear a beep from the woman's cell.

"I'm calling for help," the woman said. "Hold on."

The teenager's seizure has calmed some, but there's a bluish tinge to her face. I look in her open mouth and see a blockage. A chunk of ice is trapped at the back of her throat.

I reach in, grab the edge of the ice, and yank it out. The girl gasps and tries to sit up, color returning to her face.

Then my world turned upside down because I heard the

woman on her cell phone.

"... my daughter is having a seizure ..."

It was the same voice from yesterday, spoken with the same distress.

I stare at the woman. Maybe I've met her before. Could I have taken a 911 call from her?

The mother and teenager are talking to each other. The daughter is crying as she explains how the ice from her Freddo had been. Somehow, it lodged behind her mouth, and she couldn't breathe or remove it. Then, miraculously, it righted itself. The young girl said it was as if someone had reached into her mouth and forced the ice out of position.

They hug each other. I'm about to ask the mother how we're connected when I notice them staring toward the road.

I turn to look at what has caught their attention. Someone was lying on the ground in the middle of the lane.

I think of the time and not wanting to be late for work, so I hustle down the street. I don't want to think about what the teenager said. There really wasn't any plausible explanation for herself and her mother not having seen me. I was the one who helped her breathe again.

No one spoke to me when I got to work. It was as if I was invisible. I take my chair and turn on my computer station. The screen lights up when I sit down and place my headset on. A call is already coming in.

"You've reached 911. What's the emergency?"

A distant sound came to me. The whoosh of cars again, but this time slower. Then I heard the woman's voice.

"I didn't really see what happened. I was trying to call 911."

It all becomes clear to me.

I was the one hit by the pickup truck.

The last moments of my life were being replayed for me so I could see that I had passed. Why I refused to comprehend this before now confuses me. It even makes sense how my supervisor ignored me. He looked at my coworkers and talked about how my computer had a mind of its own. The original 911 call was trying to get me back to the location of the accident that took me.

The strange sensation of being pulled. Questions milling in my head.

I helped save that girl, yet they couldn't see me.

My computer screen is blank. I see my desk from above.

Now, I see the roof of the building.

I shut my eyes as I'm embraced.

A Lollipop and Other Dangers

I CAN'T BELIEVE THE nerve of some people, Onalee thought.

She had signaled her intention, waited for the opening, and then turned into the gas station. No one was even close to her car. Then, out of nowhere, a large SUV jumped the curb and cut her off. Her car and the SUV came within one foot of each other.

Onalee pulled up to the parking area and stopped. She didn't need gas—it was a large coffee and something sweet for the road that she required. Maybe the coffee would help settle her nerves now that she felt rattled after that close call.

She stepped out and glanced over at the SUV.

Something was wrong. She felt it right away. A familiar buzzing stirred in her stomach. The SUV driver stared into the distance, unaware of anything around him.

Onalee studied his vehicle. The top of a child's car seat

was in the back, but no evidence of anyone else. She let her eyes move back to the driver. He was watching her now.

She turned away and entered the gas station's convenience store section. She headed to the snacks area in search of a chocolate bar. Next, she meandered to the coffee dispenser. It was one of those self-serve types where she filled her cup and went to the counter to pay.

The door to the convenience store opened. The SUV driver walked up to the attendant and slammed down cash, then turned and walked back out. The attendant counted the cash and nodded that it was all there.

The SUV driver was halfway to his vehicle already.

Something was wrong with that guy, which made her feel like she had to act on it somehow.

She advanced toward the counter and opened her wallet, watching out the window as the SUV turned onto the highway and headed north, tires squealing.

When she looked back to the attendant, he wasn't alone. A tall man in a long trench coat stood by the cigarette rack.

"That's four-fifty-eight, ma'am," the clerk said.

Onalee pulled out a five. She glanced over at the man in the trench coat. He opened his mouth and said that the child was going to be hurt.

"What child?" Onalee asked.

"Excuse me?" the clerk said, placing her bill on the side and collecting her change. "What did you say?"

Onalee stared at him. "I was talking to the guy behind you." She pointed at the cigarette rack, then realized—too late—that the clerk wouldn't be able to see the guy in the trench coat. When would she remember that the entities she saw were as clear to her as the clerk staring back at her? To people like the clerk, they were invisible.

The clerk glanced over his shoulder, then back to Onalee. The look on his face told Onalee what she already knew.

"The child is in danger," Trench Coat Man said again. "Go after him. Involve the police. Go now."

Trench Coat Man disappeared.

The last thing she wanted to do was chase after the guy in the SUV, but she was given no choice. When a child was in danger, she had to act. The other side never sent her a false message—never.

She rushed out to her car, leaving the clerk holding her change and a stunned expression. She'd completely forgotten her coffee and chocolate bar on the counter. After jumping in her car, she raced out of the gas station parking lot, merging easily onto the highway.

Then she grabbed her cell phone and called 911.

Most people would hesitate at this point. She had no grounds for calling the police. No one had done anything wrong except maybe cutting her off, but that was more of a stupid driving situation than anything one would require the law for. But with Onalee, the difference was the things she could see and feel could be trusted.

She told the dispatcher, who answered that she had been dangerously cut off and that a Nissan Pathfinder SUV was heading north on Hwy. 11 in an erratic fashion. The driver was possibly inebriated, and she'd seen a child seat in the back. She had concerns about how the vehicle was being driven, and since it was a two-lane highway, the danger of a collision was high. Onalee was told that two cruisers were in the area and would be close to the vehicle in question within minutes.

Onalee luckily caught up to the Nissan within ten minutes and followed from a short distance. She silently prayed that the danger would be delayed long enough for the police to stop the SUV.

Another five minutes passed before two police cruisers pulled up fast on Onalee's tail. She moved to the right to allow them room to pass. They got around her quickly and turned on their overhead lights. The Nissan's brake lights lit up as he pulled over.

"Now what?" she said to herself. "What if nothing's wrong and he carries on?"

They would speak with the driver. Then they would see that there's nothing wrong and let him go.

At that time, she hoped the danger would come because if it didn't, she would be useless to stop it as she didn't know where it was supposed to come from in the first place.

Therefore, she had to get involved because delaying the Nissan driver from leaving too soon gave her more time to assess everything.

She pulled over behind the cop cars and exited her vehicle. Two of the three officers were already talking to the driver. The third one had held back. He noticed Onalee and headed her way.

"Are you the one who called us, ma'am?"

"Yes, I am."

"Are you okay? Did he hit your car or cause—"

Someone shouted, interrupting the officer. One of the cops was running back to his cruiser. Onalee watched with her mouth open as he flipped his lights on and cranked the siren. The cruiser's tires squealed, and he was off.

"What the hell is going on?" she asked.

Then she understood why.

About half a kilometer up the road, a large transport weaved back and forth across the lanes. He was headed in their direction. The rig traveled on the wrong side of the road for a long time.

If anyone had been going toward it, they would have been in a head-on collision.

Onalee watched as the lights and siren did their magic. The transport driver gained control of his machine, shifted gears, and pulled over onto the shoulder. In less than a minute, the situation was diffused.

She had to assume the rig must have been dangerous for the SUV driver, and that was probably why Trench Coat Man asked for the police to be involved, so their sirens would wake the driver and stop that rig from hurting anyone.

The officers still on site weren't paying much attention to the driver of the Nissan, so she decided to speak with him. He'd gotten out of his SUV and was pacing back and forth beside it.

One officer sat in the remaining cruiser, tapping into a laptop affixed to his dash.

She got as far as the back window of the SUV, which had been rolled down. Inside, a small boy was strapped into the car seat, sleeping, his head bowed slightly to the left. She went to look away and speak to the driver when something odd caught her eye.

A white stick protruded from the boy's mouth. Was that

good parenting to let a child sleep with a sucker in their mouth?

Then she looked closer at the color of the little boy's face. He'd turned a shade of purple.

"Officer!" she screamed. "I need help here!"

Onalee lunged for the back door handle, ripped it open, and grabbed the safety strap, holding the boy in place. For an annoying second, it stuck. Then it snapped open, and the child was free.

He was a dead weight in her arms. She got out and put the child on the pavement behind the Nissan. The father asked what the hell she thought she was doing.

The cop knelt beside her. "Ma'am, step aside," he ordered. "It's okay, I'm trained for this."

He knelt and put his ear to the boy's open mouth. Then, abruptly, he grabbed the boy, spun him around, and held him in a reverse bear hug. The cop locked his arms together and rammed them upward below the boy's chest plate, performing the Heimlich maneuver.

A tiny brown ball shot out of the boy's mouth, and he gasped for air. Then he cried as color returned to his face.

The father dropped to his knees, crying and saying the boy's name over and over.

Onalee learned that the father had given his son a sucker to keep him occupied while daddy talked to the policemen. It had a gum at the center, which got stuck, and the boy couldn't get it unstuck on his own.

The sucker was supposed to be a surprise for when they got home, as Daddy had been upset with his visitation rights, which was the cause of the anger Onalee had seen at the gas station.

Lucky for him, the mistake was discovered on the side of the highway by someone well-versed in the Heimlich maneuver.

If the other side would only be more specific, Onalee thought, shaking her head.

She could've stopped the guy at the gas station and told him about the gum-centered sucker beforehand.

But then, the officers were in the right place at the right time for that runaway truck.

She shrugged as she got back on the highway. We're all supposed to live and learn.

Her job was not to question how or why messages were sent to her.

She was just supposed to help where she could.

And today, she could.

Cleaning House

I PEEKED FROM BEHIND the curtain to look at my neighbor's house across the street. Every morning, for as long as I could remember, Evelyn and her husband Bart would be out doing their gardening. Or they'd at least be out having tea on their porch before they started their work in the garden.

But not today.

I edged away from the front window and headed to the door. It was time to find out what happened last night. Some neighbors call me a busybody behind my back, but I don't care.

Evelyn and her husband had been expecting a visitor to arrive around nine p.m. for a house cleaning. They'd been nervous due to the visit's odd hour and what Bart had said.

He'd talked about the woman and how strange she was. Something about her looking at empty kitchen chairs and conversing with them. Bart didn't want to admit it, but after a certain amount of prodding by Evelyn and me, he told us he thought he saw the empty chair move like someone was sitting in it.

Five minutes later, I stood at the end of their driveway in front of their house. The curtains were drawn, windows shut. The house had a kind of spooky aura that gave me shivers. I couldn't explain it. I think the only time this happened in the past was when two of their five children were killed in a car accident out on the county road. But that was so long ago.

Evelyn and Bart bought their house at the turn of the century. I never forgot this because I bought mine the same year. We all became best friends instantly. My husband passed away in the 1940s, but I lived on for my kids. I would never leave them. I think that's why Evelyn and I got along so well because of our undying connection to our children. We were the only mothers on the block who were given the nurturing gene. We raised our kids in a house of love. A piece of us is always with them, still raising and watching over them. Neither one of us would ever abandon our children.

I stand at their front door now and knock.

No one answers. I knock again. Still no answer.

I move from the porch and stop near the end of the driveway to see the entire house.

Then the front door opened, and a woman stepped out—a woman I'd never seen before. She has a candle in her hand.

What's she doing holding a candle in the bright morning sun?

"Hello," she calls to me. "Would you please come here for a moment? I would like to talk with you."

I remain standing where I am. Could this be the visitor Evelyn and Bart had over last night? If it is, what's she still doing here?

"Can you hear me?" the woman asks.

What kind of question is that? Of course, I could hear her. I'm only at the end of the driveway.

I nod.

"Good. Would you be willing to talk to me?"

Another woman stepped up behind the stranger with the candle. She looks out to the road and scans the immediate area. Her eyes move right over me, then back again. It was like she was trying *not* to see me. That's so rude and unladylike.

Both women stand on the porch, mumbling to each other. I find the courage to talk.

"What are you doing in Evelyn and Bart's house?"

Candle Woman looks directly at me. "This house belongs to Mary Howden," she says as she gestures at the woman beside her.

That's impossible. I cross my arms and tap my foot. I want to show them I'm losing my patience when I'm actually hiding my nervousness. Something is wrong here. I can feel it.

"Evelyn and her husband bought that house when I bought mine," I shout back. "We've been neighbors for as long as I can remember."

"What year did you buy your house?" Candle woman asks.

I had to think about it. I knew it was around the turn of the century, but the specific year eluded me. I decided on a guess. "Around 1904."

"And what year is this?"

What a weird question. What year is this? I can tell that Candle Woman isn't right in the head.

She starts down the porch steps, raises the candle high, and asks me to look at it. Then she repeats her question about the year.

What pulls my eye from the mesmerizing candlelight is the woman still standing on the porch, who deliberately tried not to see me standing in the driveway.

She waves frantically as she jumps from the porch and heads toward the driveway. I looked over at what had caught her attention. A little boy on a tricycle is wheeling toward me. He ambles right up next to me before he stops. Our eyes met, and he asked me where I lived.

"Right over there." I point.

The woman grabs the little boy and lifts him off the tricycle. He looks back at me with a frown. "But my friend Mike lives there. I've never seen you before."

"Come on, Toby. Let Onalee handle this."

The woman named Mary Howden walks away with Toby, leaving me to wonder who Mike is.

I turn to Candle Woman and ask if Onalee is her name, but the candle is almost in my face. She mutters something like, *look into the light, look into the light.*

I step back, images of my kids flashing into my mind. My concern for the welfare of Evelyn and Bart hovers in my awareness.

What's happening to me?

My hands come up to protect my face as the woman

continues her chant, *look into the light.*

Then she tells me to go home.

I'm literally steps from my home.

No problem, I thought. *I'm gone.*

Then Onalee says something rather shocking. She tells me to go to my *real* home to meet Evelyn and Bart again. She says my husband is waiting for me, too.

Was this some kind of joke?

My existence flutters when she tells me I'm dead. The year is 2021. She says I've been dead for over forty years and that I need to go into the light.

I turn on my heels to escape the clutches of this irrational insanity and bolt into a light so bright it envelopes me. I accept its presence immediately because it's so loving and welcome, an experience I feel waft through my existence, warming my soul.

The world around me wavers, shimmering in and out of sight, but I don't care because there's an incredible sense of peace. To my astonishment, the light seems to absorb deeper into me, with each moment intensifying the sensation of ecstasy. I briefly wonder if such an experience can kill me. I have no idea what's happening, only that I wouldn't stop it for the world.

On second thought, maybe I would for my kids.

That's when I saw them. They approached me through the light that acted like a dense fog. Evelyn and Bart are behind them. My confusion is buoyed by the immense consolation I feel by just being in the presence of the light.

Onalee's words come back to me. *Look into the light. Go home. The year is 2021.*

Someone asks me what I've done with the life I was given, and then images race behind my eyes.

I understand everything now. I'd been earthbound because of my love for my children. My life review showed me how I died and how I refused to believe it. How I refused to leave my children behind without a mother—just like Bart and Evelyn had done.

Onalee wasn't a maid and wasn't cleaning houses at odd hours. She was a psychic, doing a house cleansing at night when the candlelight would show up best to entities already on the other side.

***

Onalee set down her pen. A part of her journal writing was a recanting of a spirit and its journey home. She took a Kleenex and wiped her eyes.

One day, she would write a book about her adventures. All the things she saw in the future, the people she'd saved, and the entities she'd helped get home.

Until then, she would continue to use her gift in the name of hope.

Dinner Proposal

"So, what do you think? Will she like it?"

"I think Adrianna will love it. The question is, are you ready for this? I mean, come on, Alex, are you really ready to marry this girl?"

Alex Rung surveyed the diamonds atop the engagement ring for a long moment before closing the lid on the black velvet case.

"Steve, we've been roommates for over five years, which means you should know me by now. School's finished in June, and we're talking about moving in together. We both know that marriage is the next logical step for us as we enter the workforce. Since it's Valentine's Day, what better time to propose?"

"As long as you're sure you know what you're doing." He paused. "Although, there is one thing I'd like to know." Steve leaned closer. "Would Adrianna take your last name?"

"We've talked about her feelings, and she said she would. Why?"

"It's just that every time someone says her name, it would sound like she'd just called on the phone. Adrianna Rung—although, it does have a nice ring to it." Steve laughed, holding his gut.

"Laugh all you want, but this is—"

The phone interrupted him. Steve answered it while Alex returned to his room to put away the ring. He hears Steve's voice resonating in disbelief about something that had happened. Curiosity made him turn around and walk back out to the living room.

Steve put the phone down and looked up. "Man, I've got some bad news. You might want to sit down for this."

The look on Steve's face cautioned Alex against thoughts that he may be joking.

Steve nodded at the phone. "That was Bruno, the bartender. You might remember him from biology class in high school."

"Yeah, I've bumped into him two or three times in the last few years. Doesn't he work at Marco's Lounge out on 32nd Street?"

"That's him."

"Come to think of it, Adrianna said she was going there last night. She was meeting friends for a few drinks. Did something happen?"

Steve sat back and clasped his hands together. "That's why Bruno called. He had four ladies in last night, creating quite a ruckus. Apparently, three of them could have been

charged for lewd conduct. He thinks two of the four ladies'
names were Michelle and Tracy. They ended up leaving with
two guys from the billiard room. It was the other two that
concerned him. Valerie something or other, and one Adrianna
Miles. He said he got their names out of the guy that
Adrianna was with." Steve paused, staring at Alex. "Since
he'd heard from me that you were seeing someone with that
same name, he thought he'd call. He wanted to know if you
were with Adrianna at the bar last night. Because if it was, he
said he wouldn't have recognized you from high school. The
other thing he said was that Valerie seemed to be the only
angel among the group. She kept trying to get her friends
under control."

"Is this a joke? Straight up. Just tell me because this is
too serious to be fucking around."

Shaking his head back and forth, Steve said, "No joke,
man."

"Gimme Bruno's phone number."

"What? You don't believe me?"

"It's not that. I'll need identification that he actually saw
my Adrianna with another guy before I propose tonight."

Steve relinquished the phone number, and a plan was
quickly established.

***

Alex left the engagement ring behind. After everything
he'd heard from Bruno, it didn't look like he would be
proposing to his girlfriend. Dejected, he trudged to his beat-
up Toyota and drove to Adrianna's house, where he picked

her up on time. Alex was perceptive enough to notice that Adrianna seemed quite nervous. On any other occasion, he would have reason to ask why she wasn't acting her usual, calm self, but he already knew some of what she'd done last night.

When they got underway, Alex said, "Steve called and asked me to drop off his house keys before we head to dinner."

"Are we going back to your place?"

"He called from Marco's Lounge. We're heading there to drop them off, then we'll go to dinner."

Even in the dim light of the car, Alex saw her blanch at the mention of Marco's Lounge.

They arrived without further conversation. Alex persuaded Adrianna to at least follow him to the door where she could be polite by waving to Steve. Explaining something about not liking this place, Adrianna waited just inside the front door while Alex walked to the bar.

Steve saw Alex coming and turned to the bartender, gesturing with his ring finger. They planned for the bartender to get a positive ID of the girl Alex was supposed to marry.

Bruno glanced up and saw Alex, then looked past him to Adrianna standing by the door. By the time Alex reached Steve and handed him the house keys, Bruno had turned back to the two of them. He was shaking his head repeatedly, signaling *No* to the ring finger.

Alex read that as *don't marry her.*

With a sickness brewing in his stomach, Alex meandered back to Adrianna, and they continued to the restaurant.

On the way there, he tried to keep a straight face, fighting back the tears. How would he be able to say goodbye after four years? How could he? He couldn't believe she would sleep around on him. He knew her, trusted her.

This was shaping up to be one of the toughest things he would ever have to do, and it was on the night he had planned to propose, which only made it seem much worse. The love he felt for Adrianna was his entire world. His hopes and dreams, his future, all involved her. But now, he was destined to be alone.

They were seated in a relatively quiet area where candles were lit and wine poured. Alex decided he wouldn't be able to if he didn't say something soon.

"Adrianna, I've got something I'd like to discuss."

She set down her menu and smiled the same smile that had won his heart. "I've also got something to talk to you about."

"You go first," Alex offered, giving him a reprieve of a few minutes—more time to muster his courage for what must be done.

"No. I insist that you say your piece."

"Okay, fine." *So much for the reprieve.* "I've been thinking about us, and ..."

"Yeah? And?" Adrianna prodded.

"Well, I've been thinking—"

His cell phone chirped to the ringtone of "Stairway to Heaven." He held up his index finger for her to wait a moment while he took the call.

It was Steve. "He was wrong, man. He was wrong."

"What're you talking about?" Alex whispered. He turned sideways in his chair, angling away from Adrianna.

"When you came into the bar earlier," Steve said in a rushed tone," and I showed Bruno my ring finger, I was telling him that the girl at the door was the one you wanted to marry. When he shook his head, I thought he was saying, don't marry her."

"That's what I thought, too." Alex snuck a glance at Adrianna, who was staring off into the distance.

"But that's wrong. He shook his head because he was trying to tell us that the girl at the door wasn't the bad one last night. The names must have gotten mixed up. He thought the girl you were with was Valerie. Bruno said two minutes ago that the girl you were with tonight was the only rational one. The guy who the real Valerie was with must have gotten their names mixed up."

"Oh, man." Alex glanced up at the ceiling, then back to the floor. "I should've known. I didn't even bring *it* with me," he whispered into the phone. "Everything's so messed up now. Look, Steve, I gotta go."

Alex hung up and turned back to Adrianna.

"Everything okay?" she asked.

"Couldn't be better. Listen, I—"

Adrianna raised her hand for silence. "What I have to say can't wait any longer."

Alex nodded. "Go ahead then." It would allow him to breathe since he felt like the wind had been knocked from him.

Adrianna leaned forward. "Remember my girlfriends and I went out last night? We went out to celebrate my decision. They all got a little crazy, so I didn't feel comfortable at Marco's earlier. We were celebrating my decision to break with tradition."

"What tradition?"

Adrianna got up from her chair and moved to stand in front of Alex. "I want to ask you to marry me." She lowered to one knee before him, then took his hand. "You've given me the best four years of my life. Alex Rung, on bended knee, I ask you to be my husband. I want to carry our children, raise a family, and spend the rest of my waking days with you. You are the closest thing to heaven on earth for me, and I will never let you go. Alex, will you marry me?"

Emotions as convoluted as the ones coursing through Alex would have put a tornado to shame. Here was the woman of his dreams, moments away from being accused of wrongdoing just seconds ago, close to losing everything he had, asking *him* to marry *her*.

He felt guilty for entertaining any idea that she wouldn't have been faithful, but another part of him was elated that not only were they to remain together, but together they would remain as Mrs. and Mr. Rung.

Dreams do come true, Alex thought as he said yes, hugged her, and wept in her arms.

***

Note: the similarity of names in this story (and others), like Alex and Bruno, were the basis of the names found in the Sarah Roberts novels. Although each character is an individual, their likeness is connected in name only.

Foretold

When I held the bus ticket out, I saw my hand shaking. I consciously moved it enough to conceal the tremors from the bus driver. I didn't realize this journey would be so hard on my nerves. That was why I was taking the trip in the first place, so that I wouldn't have a nervous breakdown.

After pulling out my novel, I stuffed my duffel bag under the seat and settled for the four-hour ride to Toronto. My stomach protested as the bus driver closed the door, signaling that we would be underway momentarily. That confirmed to me just how nervous I really was.

Then, the oddest thing happened. I looked out the bus window and saw a woman staring at me. At least it looked like she was watching me. I pulled my gaze away from her. No one was sitting two seats ahead or behind me, so she *had* to've been looking at me.

When I turned back, she was gone.

The bus driver opened the door, and the woman got on. She handed her ticket to the driver and started down the aisle. I stared out the window to avoid meeting her gaze. I wasn't in the mood to talk, even though I had no idea her intentions.

The bus got underway. Even though I brought my novel, I couldn't concentrate, so I stowed it back in my bag as the woman sat across from me. She smiled when I looked at her. I turned away and angled myself toward the window.

I closed my eyes. When I opened them again, I could tell we were about fifteen minutes away from our first stop in Bracebridge. I must've slept for the first leg of the trip south.

"Heading to Toronto?" the woman asked.

I nodded. "You?" It was a feeble attempt to be social.

She shook her head. "Bracebridge. I'm getting off in a few minutes. Any specific reasons for Toronto?"

I didn't want to talk about it. Actually, I didn't want to talk at all. She had watched me from outside the bus and then got on and sat near me. I talked for a few minutes to see what her game was since she'd be getting off the bus soon.

"Real estate."

"You mean you're looking to move to Toronto?"

"No. My childhood house is up for sale."

"Your childhood house? Wow. Must be seriously attached to it. Or is there some other reason?"

"It's a long story." I realized that this was going nowhere. "Do I know you or something?"

"No, I don't think so."

"Then, if you don't mind, I'm just going to recline back and read."

"I'm not trying to hit on you. I see the wedding ring." She adjusted herself in the seat to aim her body directly at me. "You look like a man who would have two kids and a loving wife. I can tell that you're nervous about something. I think you're so nervous that you chose to take the bus to Toronto instead of driving yourself."

She hit the nail on the head. I *had* decided just last night to take the bus. This trip to Toronto was about closure. I knew tears were coming within the next twelve hours, and I didn't want to be alone when they came, driving in the dark.

My eyes widened as the mystery woman continued talking.

"You look like a Steve or a Mike, but I would bet your name is …" She paused and looked at the seat beside her. No one was there. "Jake."

I jolted with surprise. There's no way someone could guess my name like that. *Impossible*. "You do know me, don't you?"

She reached across the aisle to shake my hand. "My name is Onalee, and I've never met you before. It's just that sometimes I can get perceptive."

I took her proffered hand and shook it.

"Perceptive? Sounds more like psychic to me." I moved my head back and forth at the surprise I felt. This encounter had gone from weird to strange, and I was going crazy.

"Tell me about the house. Are you looking to buy it or just want to see it?"

Against my wishes, I spoke just above a whisper. "I want to look at it."

"Is there something particular you're looking for?"

"An accident happened when I was ten that I don't think I completely dealt with. My wife and I felt this was a good opportunity to revisit the house, walk through the rooms, and flood my senses by merging my past to the here and now." I shook my head. "Something like that."

"If whatever happened was that tragic to still be with you emotionally, then I agree with your assessment that you should go. And I'm sure your mother would be happy for you."

I sat up in my seat. *Unbelievable.* She could not know that this had anything to do with my mother.

"How could you know this relates to my mother?"

"Well, it would make sense that when you were ten, she would have been with you through the difficult time. I just figured she's involved."

I watched the woman stand. Then I realized the bus was stopping. We were in Bracebridge.

The woman turned around and leaned closer. Her voice changed. It lowered and deepened.

"Your mother wants me to tell you that she has always loved you and is so sorry for the pain it caused. She said that if she could've done it any other way, the good Lord knows she would've. Take the blame off your shoulders, Jake Matthew. Enjoy your children as much as you can for her because she didn't get to."

Then the woman walked away and out of my life, my mouth open.

The pain came up, and the tears followed.

I hid in the bus seat and wept.

The thing is, my mother had been dead for fifteen years.

***

I stood on the street before my childhood residence, emotions stirring again. I almost turned around and left. This house was the only earthly structure with physical control over my limbs. The horror I caused when I was ten has never left my thoughts. The pain my mother went through, the disfigurement.

A shadow crossed the living room window. My appointment with the agent started five minutes ago, but no car was in the driveway. Could she be here already?

I walked up the front steps before stopping myself, rang the bell, and twisted the doorknob. The foyer was exactly as I remembered it, except now it was bare. The previous owners had already vacated.

Scratching noises came from the kitchen area.

I scanned the foyer, took it all in, and then moved toward the kitchen.

Memories flooded me. Christmases with Dad before he died when I was nine. Riding my first bike through this very hallway. Coloring the kitchen walls with crayons. Of course, getting into lots of trouble, too. The list went on and on.

A woman was on her hands and knees scrubbing the floor near the kitchen sink.

"Hello," I said softly so as not to startle her.

She didn't turn around or look up. "Hello, Jake. Here to see the house?" Her tone was upbeat and happy.

"Yes. Are you the real estate agent?"

"Not exactly. But I heard about you coming and wanted

to clean up the place."

"Are you the seller?"

"Let's just say I am interested in selling this house. Was your journey pleasant?"

"Odd. I would call it odd. But otherwise, okay." I turned toward the stove. It looked like someone had taken the time to cover the stain. The acid had eaten through the wallpaper and the drywall all those years ago. It had been rebuilt, but there would always be a shadow in my eyes.

"You know, it wasn't your fault," the woman said. "I heard what happened here when you were ten, and I can tell you it wasn't your fault."

Immediately, I became defensive. Who was this woman? And how could she know that information? I hadn't said a word to the agent.

"The acid was planted there by accident," the woman continued. "Your mother found it and figured out what it was right away. She was coming back into the kitchen to dispose of it when you happened to be climbing onto the counter."

This woman knew more than anyone did. Watching her arms stop scrubbing the floor as she talked was maddening. I stood behind her, paralyzed in shock, awe, and wonder. This day was like a visit to *The Outer Limits*, so why not go to *The Twilight Zone*, too?

"We both know you were not allowed to sneak cookies, but you thought your mother was indisposed. She entered the kitchen quickly and screamed your name because you were right beside the pot of acid. And we both know that when you turned and tried to drop to the floor, your arm hit the pot's handle, causing it to flip and spew into your mother's face.

Now, you must accept it was a complete accident and let it go."

I needed to sit down. I was speechless. No one had said these exact words to me—ever.

My mother lost her job because no one wanted to work with someone so disfigured. Three years later, she died of despair. I spent several years in foster homes. But all those years, I lived in a personal private jail because deep down inside, I believed I killed my mother.

"But you didn't kill her," the woman said. "Her death was a matter of fate."

The stranger had read my mind.

"What's going on here?"

She stopped scrubbing the floor and got to her feet.

When she turned around to face me, I would swear on a stack of Bibles that the woman four feet from me in the kitchen of my childhood house was my mother, unmarred. She looked exactly as I remembered her before I turned ten.

"What's going on …?" I tried to repeat, but emotion choked off my throat.

"I wanted to come by today to tell you that it's okay. Let it out. I'm happy. Look at my face and remember me like this. Because this is how I really am. You didn't kill me, Jake, and you need to stop torturing yourself. My body may have died, but I didn't. Don't allow yourself to remain dead on the inside."

The sound of a knock cut her off.

"Hello!" someone called from the front door.

I turned at the sound and then looked back to where my mother had been standing—but she was gone. The water in my eyes thwarted my every move as I exited my childhood house. The real estate agent was ten minutes late and didn't try to stop me as I hustled past her.

I'm alive, and I thank God for the proof.

The hell I created was in me, and it's time to purge it, move on, and start living again.

I got what I came for.

Closure.

Lost and Found

What mattered most was the heat. Without it, he would surely die.

Peter Hall couldn't remember a hiking trip where the cold had taken such a tight grip as this one had. He couldn't feel his feet for at least the last half hour. The numbness that had set in cost him the ability to bend his toes. With each step, Peter thought he resembled a penguin.

Seven hours before, the sun shining in the midday sky, he had decided to hike into the mountains surrounding his cabin. He left his snowshoes behind because he wouldn't need them. This year, they had seen the least snowfall in the area since the 1940s.

Trudging along to the mouth of the path that would lead him to the river, Peter reveled in the peace. He was far enough away from civilization that he couldn't detect the sound of an engine from an automobile or a plane. Not a single sound, but nature.

After an hour, Peter was surprised to see what looked like an old footpath he'd never seen in his seven years at the cabin. Curious about where this undiscovered route would take him, he wandered through a small thicket of brush and started a new journey. Having meandered along the thin path for over half an hour, he decided to continue this venture another day as the sun would soon set. It left him just enough time to return to the river and the familiar trail that led back to his cabin.

The problems began when he tried to retrace his steps. He found it peculiar that his footprints in the snow had disappeared in less than five minutes. There hadn't been any new snow, and it wasn't obvious they'd been brushed over. They were just gone as if no one had parted the snow in the first place.

After ten minutes, the trail itself disappeared. A dead tree lay in the middle of where the path was supposed to go. Looking to either side of it, nothing resembled a path.

He was lost.

Completely bewildered, Peter had to succumb to the notion that he had taken a wrong turn on the way back, which he found odd because he was an experienced tracker with an incredible sense of direction. Either way, whether he had been daydreaming or simply had a mental lapse of his surroundings, he was somewhere in the middle of nowhere, with no idea which way to go or which not to go.

Time didn't stop, though. The sun had disappeared, the temperature had dropped, and the snow underfoot hardened in the colder night temperature. Cursing himself for not being properly dressed for such an excursion, he waddled along, hoping to find some kind of shelter for the remainder of the evening.

The only heat left in his body came from his breath, which couldn't seem to lend any to his hands as he blew on them. He quickly realized that he was in danger of freezing to death, so he went about clumping snow together to create a makeshift fort. When completely surrounded by snow, the temperature inside remained at one degree Celsius, enough to sustain life. However, he couldn't see a snow buildup large enough to burrow into. He would have to continue on the path, searching for a snowbank or a drift large enough.

He grinned at the irony. Getting out of the snowy conditions to survive contrasted with burrowing into the snow to stay alive.

After about twenty slow paces, he needed to rest. His extremities were frozen stiff, and his knee joints were not far behind. The frostbite concern was worrying him now. If he did make it out of this alive, what parts of his body would he get to keep?

He dropped beside a large pine tree and huddled his face deeper into his parka hood. His father came to mind. He hadn't thought of his dad in years. Questions like, what would Dad do now? How would he get out of this mess? Peter felt sure that if his father were here, he'd have some off-handed remark on how to get back to the cabin as if he knew the way the whole time and was saving the best for last. Or how it was all Peter's fault for getting lost in the first place.

Eventually, his weakened state and circulation problems

caused him to surrender consciousness. His head bowed, sleep came and went as more snow drifted from the darkened sky. Conditions inside and outgrew increasingly worse.

As his sleep deepened closer to a coma state, Peter had the sensation of being lifted. The part of his mind that was still aware strove hard to revive his senses. All that came from him was a soft grunt and moan. Several times, he felt that he could hear a man speaking words of consolation.

"It'll be okay. It's not your time. I'll see you when you're ready."

Words like this continued over and over. At one point, Peter felt that he had passed on and that this was what heaven felt like. Levitation combined with numbness and a soft, melodic voice whispering in his ear. He convinced himself that he must have died because the speaker started to sound more and more like his father, who had been dead for over fifteen years.

A soft thumping stirred Peter to half-consciousness, awakening him in a delirium. He realized that he was being set down onto something hard. There was a loud knocking, and then that voice again, whispering into his ear.

"You're safe now, son. These people will warm you and clothe you. I'll see you when I see you."

The sound of an old wooden door creaked open.

"Hello. Is anyone there?" A woman.

The sensation of light and warmth caressed his face.

He thought that the woman who answered the door must be carrying a lantern.

"Oh, dear. Johnson!" she bellowed. "Come quick!"

Peter was dragged, not lifted, across the shack's

floorboards toward a crackling fire. The twosome worked tirelessly, stripping his frozen clothes and covering him in warm blankets. The fire shot its warm breath his way, and life wound through his worn limbs.

After a while, he regained consciousness and mumbled thanks and gratitude for all they had done for him. He especially wanted to thank the man for carrying him from the bush.

"I didn't carry you anywhere," the man said. "As a matter of fact, I had to drag you across my floor to the fireplace. You're too heavy for me. Maybe in my youth, but not today."

"Well, then, how did I get here?" Peter asked, still shivering slightly.

"You must have walked. After taking you off the porch, I looked out to see if anyone else was with you, and I only saw one set of footprints."

"Someone carried me."

"No. It couldn't be possible because the prints match your boots."

"In my condition, I couldn't have walked."

The woman sat back in her chair. "Come to think of it, I did hear someone talking just before I opened the door. He said something like, 'I'll see you when I see you.' I thought you were mumbling, but it was too clear to've been said by you, seeing as how you're struggling to talk even now."

I'll see you when I see you was something his father always said to him when he was a child. Anytime Peter would leave the house for any reason, his dad would say those same words.

Could it be possible that his father had come to help?

The woman leaned forward. "Come to think of it, I opened the door as I heard those words, so it had to be you, talking in some kind of delirium."

"That's not possible," the old man added. "Just look at how cooperative his mouth is now. Delirium or no delirium, he couldn't have talked too clearly."

Peter recalled that his deliverer had used the term, *son*. He lay back and stared at the roof of the wooden shack as the fire raged on before him, basking him in life-saving heat. He reflected on his good fortune to have been delivered to these kind people by someone who will remain unknown. A certain someone whom Peter felt he knew. The only man who called him a son.

His last thought before sleep took him was, *I'll be seeing you when I see you, Dad.*

The Phone Call

HE HATED THE RINGTONE his wife had selected: a shrill chirp that made him jump every time it rang. He grabbed the closest hands-free in the hallway and snapped, "Hello" into the receiver.

"Is that any way to answer a phone?"

He recognized his mother's voice immediately.

"No, it's just that I'm putting Matthew to bed. I wasn't sure who'd be calling at this hour."

"I wanted to wish Joan good luck in court tomorrow," his mother said. "I know she's working long hours on this case, and we've talked a couple of times about how stressed out she is with this one."

"Joan left an hour ago, headed for the office. She wanted to go over some final preparations before the morning. After I put Matthew to bed, I would call her because she had forgotten her purse. I'll let her know you called."

"Can you put Matthew on the phone? I'd like to say goodnight to him."

Mike ushered his son to the living room, where he sat and giggled for ten minutes while talking to his grandmother. It gave Mike a chance to clean the dishes in the kitchen. He didn't expect Joan back until eleven or twelve, but if she surprised him and came home early, he wanted everything looking reasonably tidy.

Matthew stepped into the kitchen a few moments later and handed him the phone.

"Grandma said goodbye and hung up."

Mike walked his son to his room. After the usual delays, he got Matthew settled down and sleepy enough that his eyelids looked heavy.

His watch said 9:32 p.m.

An hour or two until Joan comes home.

He had just exited Matthew's room when the phone rang again. He hustled down the hall and checked call display on the hands-free—no number.

He hit "Talk" and put the phone to his ear.

"Mike, it's me."

"Joan?" It could be his wife, but her voice sounded tinny and distant like she was calling from inside an empty warehouse.

"Put Matthew on the phone. I want to say goodnight. I need to hear his voice."

What was it with everyone suddenly wanting to say goodnight to Matthew? He seemed to be quite the popular four-year-old boy.

"He's already asleep. I wouldn't want to wake him."

"He's not sleeping. He will call your name in a few seconds, looking for water. You forgot to put his glass of water next to his bed."

Mike frowned, his gaze moving to the counter where Matthew's glass of water still sat.

"Okay, that's weird. How could you know something like that? Also, unless you're in the house, you wouldn't know what Matthew will be doing in—"

His son called him from down the hallway. He asked for his water.

Mike was stunned. He didn't hear a thing from his wife—he couldn't even hear her breathing—the line sounded dead until she spoke.

"I love you so much, Mike. Walk to him and put him on, okay?"

Stunned into silence, that's what he did. At least, that's how he remembered it. A zombie-like walk down the narrow hallway of their upscale condo. Turning to the left into his son's bedroom, he kneels to hand Matthew the phone.

While they talked, his mind raced to figure out how Joan could know their son would ask for a drink. That was *psychic* weird. And coming from a woman who hates anything and everything remotely psychic. In fact, Joan made jokes about organized religion and spirituality. She was a proud atheist.

She couldn't know what was happening without installing cameras and listening devices in the house.

He glanced down as Matthew handed him the phone. When he placed it to his ear, he heard nothing.

"Hello?"

No response. No one was there.

He looked back at his four-year-old son, who lay in bed, fast asleep. It appeared as if he hadn't been awakened, thoughts of a drink of water long gone.

Mike stepped from the room and looked at the clock in the kitchen.

11:02 p.m.

How the hell did he lose an hour?

Then he remembered that Joan had forgotten her purse. He grabbed the phone and checked the last number. It showed his mother but not his wife.

It was as if Joan hadn't called at all.

He ran for his Rolodex and flipped to her office number. Staff were still in the legal library. Someone could direct him to where his wife was.

But when he called, the night security said she hadn't been in. She needed to swipe her card for access after-hours, but Joan's card hadn't been used all night. The security officers' computer system hadn't registered her entering or leaving.

So then, where was she, and where did she call from? He decided to try her cell phone. After dialing, he heard it ringing in their bedroom. She must've left it, too, sitting on the charger.

He had no way of getting a hold of her. He would just have to wait until she came home.

He poured himself a glass of red wine and stumbled over to the couch. The television had nothing interesting on it but news at that hour. He leaned back on the sofa as the local news featured another car accident on the highway. A four-car pile-up involving two SUVs. One brown Laredo, and—

Mike leaned forward, staring at the TV screen. His wife drove a brown Laredo. She had a Baby On Board sign in the back window, and so did this one.

He stood up. The phone rang. He grabbed the hands-free. Call display said it was Liberty Memorial Hospital.

"Hello," he barked into the phone.

"We're looking for a Mr. Joshua."

"That would be me," Mike said as his stomach dropped and his mind shouted *no* repeatedly.

"We would have called sooner, but your wife had no identification. I'm Dr. Matheson from Liberty Memorial."

Mike thought about the purse she'd left behind. The cell phone with pre-programmed numbers is still sitting on the charger.

"What's happened?" Mike asked. "Is my wife okay?"

"Your wife was in a car accident. She'll be fine, though. The only injury she sustained was a hit on the head. She was unconscious when she arrived at the hospital. At this point, it looks like she'll be okay. However, something strange happened. She went into cardiac arrest around nine-thirty this evening. At one point, we weren't sure if we would lose her. There's no need to worry, though. She's out of danger now. We'll need to keep her here for observation overnight."

"I'm coming down there to see her. Is she awake?"

"That's how we found out who she was and got your phone number."

"I'll be there in fifteen minutes."

Mike hung up and slipped his shoes on. He ran to the condo next door and knocked lightly.

"Mike?" Barbara asked, opening the door. "It's late. What's going on?"

"Joan's in the hospital. I'm needed there. Can you watch TV in my condo until I return in an hour? Eat or drink whatever you want."

"What happened to Joan?"

"Barbara, I need to leave. Can you?"

"Well, I was going to call this an early night—"

"I'll pay you one hundred dollars for one hour."

"On second thought—let me get my keys."

Barbara slipped back into her apartment.

Mike bolted for the elevators and, fifteen minutes later, was inside the hospital. He found the doctor who had called him and asked for a moment with him.

"When can I talk to her?" Mike asked.

"There's one thing I should tell you." The doctor edged off to the side of the corridor and leaned his shoulder on the wall.

"What's that?" Mike's breathing grew erratic.

"Your wife had a heart attack. There was a moment during the heart attack where your wife was clinically dead for at least two minutes. We tried everything, but her heart wouldn't start pumping on its own during that time. Just when we thought there was nothing else we could do, her heart woke up like it was sleeping or something. Strangest thing ever."

"And she's fine now?"

The doctor nodded. "She's completely fine, and luckily, there appears to be no lasting damage. She's quite lucid. She's able to talk for herself and think for herself."

"So, can I talk to her?"

"She's right in there." The doctor pointed at room 203.

Mike strode over and entered the room.

Joan lay on the hospital bed, tears slipping from her eyes.

They embraced, Mike handling her gently.

"I'm so happy you're okay," he whispered.

"Mike," she said.

He eased back and stared down at her.

"Mike, I left my body and floated above the doctors as they worked to revive me. Apparently, it happened just after 9:30 p.m."

"When you called me, but how's that possible?"

"I wanted to hear your voices one more time before I left this place, but someone on the other side pushed me back, saying I had unfinished business here."

She looked away, wiping her eyes.

Mike just gawked at her.

"Honey." Their eyes met. "I died and saw the other side. It was so peaceful, so warm and loving. I don't know how to describe it in words." She sniffled and caught her breath. After a moment, she continued. "It felt like home. There was a pulling sensation and an internal desire to let go and be pulled. But I couldn't go. I couldn't leave you alone with Matthew. I love you both so much."

They embraced again, and Mike knew his wife was no longer a proud atheist.

A Greater Justice

There was nothing he wouldn't do or at least try once. But meeting with a psychic was something he had never considered. His wife had pushed for it ever since Joshua died last year. She'd been worried that the same fate would be cast upon them, and she wanted to be sure they were safe.

Like anyone can predict the future, Jerry thought as Ashley pulled on the door and entered the psychic's home.

"Good evening."

Jerry turned and almost laughed. The psychic stood behind him wearing an ugly green sweater, three different chains around her neck, and stupid earrings that did some kind of multiple-loop thing. She was definitely a smoker. No one could have that many wrinkles and not have benefitted from the help of a healthy carcinogen.

He stepped back, maintaining his composure.

Ashley extended her hand. "Pleased to meet you," she said.

"I'm sorry." The psychic moved backward a few inches. "I don't touch people. Only when doing readings."

Ashley lowered her hand. Jerry saw the awkwardness, the embarrassment on her face.

The psychic woman didn't offer to take their jackets or show them to a table. All she did was stare at Jerry. He looked back at her, his eyes unwavering. Many men had stared him down in darker corners than this. He'd almost killed a man in prison six months ago because of this exact kind of disrespect. He wasn't about to wink, let alone look away.

But the psychic blinked. A chill or something made her shoulders vibrate. Then, as if that spurred her on, she walked past the two of them.

He looked at Ashley and thought, *where the hell did you find this five-foot crazy bitch?*

"Please," the psychic said. "Follow me."

"What the fuck was that all about?" Jerry whispered to Ashley.

She smacked his arm. "Please. Try to behave."

"This is fucked. If she disrespects me again, I'm done. Got that? No fucking around. I don't even want to be here."

"I know." Ashley faced him and gripped both his arms. "Do this for me. Please. We'll be out of here in thirty minutes."

Jerry nodded. Fine. Fuck it.

Ashley moved away. He blew out a calming breath and followed her down the hall.

The psychic had set up a fancy table with five chairs in the kitchen, all evenly spread out except for the head chair. It sat at least three feet from any other.

She really doesn't like to be touched.

Incense burned in every corner of the room. It was almost enough to make Jerry gag.

How the hell am I supposed to breathe in here?

He reached into his breast pocket and produced his cigarette pack. With the deft ability of a lifetime smoker, he flipped open the top, jolted the pack with the snap of his wrist, causing one cigarette to rise above the rest, and clamped his lips onto it.

"No smoking in here," the psychic said.

Ashley tapped his arm. "Jerry, please."

"What?" He raised his shoulders and extended both hands. "There's so much smoke in here already. Explain how one little cancer stick will matter. Seriously."

Ashley looked at him with her pleading eyes, her chin lowered, eyebrows raised. She knew it was the one look that always melted him.

"Okay, okay. But this shit is starting to piss me off. Now, on with the show."

He grabbed a chair, pulled it out, and plunked down hard.

Ashley looked at the psychic. "I'm sorry. Jerry doesn't believe in psychics. If you want, you can still do a reading for him as planned, but really, he's just here to support me. Will that still be okay?"

The psychic eased her chair out and slowly sat on it. Everything seemed calculated and precise. Either she had a major OCD complex, or she was just fucked.

What bothered Jerry the most was how she wouldn't look at him. Ever since the prolonged stare in the hallway, she had avoided all eye contact.

"I understand. Such is the nature of my gift. Let us begin, shall we?"

Ashley nodded and snuck a look at Jerry. He pursed his lips and sliced a grim smile across his face.

The psychic reached for a remote control sitting on the counter beside her. She touched some buttons, and the lights in the kitchen dimmed. She took a pair of sunglasses from the same counter and placed them on her head.

Then she mumbled to herself.

Jerry fought an internal urge to stand and walk out. The only thing that stopped him was the aftermath. Ashley would be so pissed the whole night would be ruined, and sex would be out of the question. Ashley knew he was ready to bolt. She placed a calming hand on his knee under the table and squeezed softly. What was meant as a reassuring gesture only added to his urge to leave.

Sitting in a darkened kitchen filled with incense smoke, watching a psychic mutter to herself while wearing a green sweater and stupid sunglasses, only added to his agitation. When Ashley touched him under the table, he almost shouted in surprise.

The psychic's head lifted. She appeared to be staring straight ahead at nothing.

What the fuck is this now?

"I'm sorry," she began. "Excuse my mumbling. I always ask to be surrounded by clean spirits. Sometimes emotionally charged entities can disturb our time together." She placed her right hand on the table, palm up. Then she did the same with her left. "I will only be able to accept half my usual fee."

Ashley looked at Jerry and then back to the psychic. "Why's that?"

"I'm sorry. I cannot do a reading for the man you have brought here today. His energy is blocking me."

The fight to hold his tongue was intense. If Ashley hadn't spoken as fast as she had, Jerry would've cussed the woman out and left, probably breaking the door on his way outside.

"Why can't you? The appointment was set for the both of us."

"I am a psychic. In order to use my gift to offer a positive reading, I committed that I would never lie to a client."

"Okay, that's noble," Ashley said. "What does that have to do with Jerry? He's not asking you to lie."

The psychic lowered her head. "Are you sure you want to hear what I have to say? You won't like it."

Ashley looked at Jerry, her face asking him to answer. He nodded. Using his mouth at that moment would only cause a disturbance, and Ashley would blame him for fucking everything up.

Shit, no matter how I look at it, I'm going to be blamed for this.

"Please tell us the problem," Ashley told the psychic.

The woman's head still faced down. She mumbled something under her breath again.

Jerry had had enough. "What was that?" he snapped.

Ashley's hand tightened on his thigh.

"I said, sometimes I hate my job."

Jerry could tell Ashley was getting scared when she

spoke again.

"Tell us, please. What's wrong with Jerry? What's going to happen to him?"

"That's the problem. I don't know."

"What do you mean you don't know?"

"I can't see a future for him after Saturday night."

Jerry exploded from the table, bumping it as he stood. "What the fuck is this? You gonna want to start talking bitch, and fast."

"Jerry!" Ashley screamed.

"No, wait," the psychic shouted. "I understand his anger."

Jerry smacked the table with the side of his hand. "You better because no one threatens me. What's supposed to happen Saturday?"

"All I see is something about a delivery truck. You are driving it. Then nothing. I don't understand it. I'm blocked from seeing more. Maybe your disbelief is locking me up."

"Oh sure, blame me after you say I'm going to die."

Ashley was crying softly now.

Bet you didn't bargain for this, did you, bitch?

"We're outta here. Let's go, Ashley."

She remained seated. "Wait, please. Is there anything else … you can tell us? What about our son, Joshua? Is he here?"

"I'm sorry. I think it's better if you both leave. The energy here has darkened, and it's now attracting negative energy."

"Is there anything Jerry can do?" Ashley wiped her eyes.

Jerry hated to see her cry. He couldn't be there anymore. He turned on his heels and stormed outside. Even before he hit the door, he had a lit cigarette in his mouth.

***

"You know as well as I do," Ashley said, "that you'll be dead before the night is over. I can't believe you'd even consider still doing this."

"Look, honey, I'm left with no choice. I don't believe in psychics. No one can tell you whether you live or die." He pulled his jacket over his shoulders and leaned against the wall. "After I do this job, we'll be able to pay the rent and buy groceries again."

Ashley wondered if this would be the final straw. Would this push her to leave after all they'd been through? She'd stayed with him during his stint in jail. She'd stayed when the collapse of their marriage looked imminent after the death of their only child. She would stay with him through anything except when he knowingly tested fate at the cost of his own life.

"I won't sit idly by and watch you kill yourself."

"What's that supposed to mean? All I have to do is drive a truck twenty kilometers away, drop it off, leave the keys in the ignition, and walk away. And for that, I get a cool ten grand. How is that suicidal in any way? Baby, we can start living again. That old weird fucking psychic didn't know what she was talking about."

"Sure she didn't. It's Saturday night. You're hired to drive a delivery truck." Ashley slapped his arm. "Come on. You're smarter than that. Even if she's wrong, you don't fuck with fate." Ashley looked away, her eyes watering.

Three years ago, they'd lost their son. Tonight, she felt

like she was losing her husband. Fierce determination to change his mind seized her. The only way to save his life was to force him to stay.

"Ever since our son had his accident, you've changed," Ashley said as tears pushed past her eyelids.

"Changed? How?"

She pulled finger after finger down as she rambled off her list of sorrow. "You lost your job. You started dealing drugs, and the problems with your drinking have almost killed you numerous times. When the police raided the factory and arrested those people for narcotics offenses, one of them had to be you. Six months in jail is a big part of your life, just gone forever. And now you want to deliver a truck for the same guys who put you in jail."

Jerry shook his head. "I don't understand you. What is illegal about driving a truck twenty kilometers? No one can arrest me for that. I'll be completely safe. It's late in the evening. Traffic will be light. I'll be extra careful."

"It's what's in the truck that scares me. You know exactly the kind of stuff these people will be shipping. The really frightening thing is that you could be risking your life, and you won't even believe it. I wish Joshua were here. He'd talk you out of it."

"None of this would be happening if Josh hadn't died. I would've never started dealing. Don't you think we both had to deal with the loss of our son in our own way? My detox program helped me understand a lot about what I was doing to handle the loss of Josh. But this job tonight can set the record straight." He snapped his fingers. "Just like that, ten thousand dollars."

"Just like that"—Ashley imitated his snap—"dead."

She moved closer to him. "Please don't do it. Stay home."

"I can't. Once you give your word to these guys, you have to keep it. There's no going back now."

"Then let's make a break for it. We've got nothing left to keep us here but bad memories and sadness—bills, too."

Jerry shook his head in an exaggerated version of no. "If they wanted to, they would find us. I have to do this last job, and I will."

He snatched up his car keys and cell phone. Ashley stopped him with her sharp words.

"Don't expect me to be here when you return." She had nothing left in her arsenal. This was the final blow.

She turned away to hide her tears. When the door slammed shut behind him, she walked to the front window and watched him moving toward his car, knowing she'd never see him alive again.

***

Jerry kept his speed down on the way to the factory. The last thing he needed was to be pulled over for speeding and then deal with the police.

The factory looked darker than usual. Most of the lights were out. As he pulled to the security gate, the door moved on its rollers to admit him. No one was there to check his badge.

He drove through and went to the back of the building, where they said the truck would be parked. Jerry walked around and tried the truck's driver's side door. It was unlocked.

He looked left and right, but the lot was empty. What if the psychic was right? What if he was supposed to die tonight?

Was this just a simple drop, or could someone hate him enough to want to kill him? Too late now for second-guessing. He was committed. He had to do it.

After starting the truck, he put it in gear and drove toward the security gate. The only movement was the heavy gate rolling back as he neared it.

Twenty kilometers to go and ten thousand dollars to spend, he thought.

He was on his way. Checking the mirrors frequently, he detected no one following him. At each red light, he stopped. In everything he did, he had to be meticulous.

The only thing that made him jump was the disturbing sound of his cell phone playing "Stan" by Eminem as it began to ring.

He momentarily fumbled in his breast pocket and then pulled out his cell phone. The call display told him it wasn't his wife.

Private caller.

"Hello?"

"Pull over immediately. Stop the truck!"

The psychic?

"What?" He pulled the phone away from his ear and looked at it as if it held answers to his questions. He jammed the phone against his head again and shouted, "What the fuck's going on? What do you know?"

"We are out of time for niceties. In less than two minutes, you will die unless you pull over and stop the truck. Do it now."

Up ahead, a stoplight had turned red about a hundred yards away. Nerves hit him hard, making his stomach drop. He decided to err on the side of caution and put on his turn signal, moving to the curb.

"Okay, I've pulled over. You've got thirty seconds to tell me why. If what you have to say doesn't fit well with me, then I will continue driving."

He sat in the truck's cab, his heart beating in his throat, and listened as the woman explained.

"I was told that you needed my help. I was told to interfere for a greater justice. Normally, I don't do this sort of thing."

"What the hell does that mean? Did my wife call you? Is she behind this?" He nodded dramatically. "Now, that would make sense. How else would you get my cell number? Oh, wait, don't answer that. You're psychic, right? Got it."

"Someone named Joshua told me."

Those words cut through him. Joshua? What was she talking about?

A stray bullet hit Joshua several years back in a park. The police never caught the asshole who did it. Jerry dropped his head, stared at his lap, and concentrated on breathing.

"This is a sick joke," he managed to mumble.

"No joke. Joshua said it wasn't your fault. You were both in the park the day he was shot. Even though it was your idea to play catch, you shouldn't blame yourself for what happened. He told me that you always said, 'Oh my gosh, look, it's Josh.' His mother disliked that, but you loved saying it when it was just the two of you."

Jerry didn't know that words could have such an effect on him. Despite the lump filling his throat, he tried to speak but couldn't.

"I can see and hear things from the other side that don't make sense," the psychic continued. "In this case, Joshua came through very strong. As we talk, he's still trying to tell me something."

For a few moments, Jerry couldn't hear anything. He scanned the mirrors and the empty road ahead, but everything remained calm.

The woman continued. "He says you're slumped over the truck wheel, idling about one hundred yards from a red light that's still red."

Jerry looked up and could see that it was, in fact, still red. "That's true."

"The light isn't defective, Jerry. The people who hired you have fixed it to stay that way. A block down on the right side of the red light, you will find a car filled with four men, each with silenced weapons. I'm being told that you are marked for execution. After your jail time, they found out that it was your son they'd killed that day at the park. They think you're working for them so that you can expose them. They want to kill you. I'm sorry. I can only tell you what I'm being told. When you came to my home, I saw you dead on Saturday. Your son is telling me how. He said I had to tell you for a greater justice."

Jerry tossed the phone onto the seat beside him and put the truck in gear. Athletes call it being in the zone. Jerry felt a calmness he hadn't felt in over a year.

A greater justice.

Of course. His son knew him. The people who hurt his baby boy were never found. They were sitting in a car a block down on the right tonight.

He drove the truck up to the red light. At the corner, he turned toward the vehicle parked on the side of the road.

Even before the car's doors had fully opened, the large truck made contact with the grill, mounting the windshield and crushing all four men below the truck's chassis.

Upon impact, Jerry's head hit the truck's windshield in an odd way, snapping his tense neck and killing him almost instantly.

His last thought was that a greater justice had been served.

His son's murderers were dead.

On the last beat of his heart, the edges of his lips curled up in a smile.

The Imprudent Son Returns

PERRY STRALL SAT UP slowly and eased his feet off the edge of the bed. He rubbed his neck and turned to stare at the empty spot where his wife should be.

The sight of the untouched side of the bed threatened to bring him to tears. They'd had forty-five years of marriage with minor arguments here and there, but never violence— never violence.

Until last night.

He wondered if Marge's injuries were serious enough to keep her at the hospital for an extended period.

He whispered a silent prayer and closed his eyes. After a moment to reflect, he mouthed a soft apology to the empty room, then stepped from the bedroom, surprised at how good he felt. His arthritic joints weren't performing their usual needlework on his nerves. He paused at the top of the stairs to swing his leg back and forth while holding the banister. His bum knee hadn't felt this strong in years.

With each step, Perry felt like a new man. He made it to the kitchen and sat down at the table.

Perry had never hit Marge before. It was an accident. He had no idea what came over him.

Maybe I'm like my wayward son?

Perry dismissed the thought. There was no way he was like his son. Elton was a killer, a murderer. Perry was the opposite. He could never hurt anyone.

Except for my own wife, evidently.

The clock on the stove said it was eleven a.m. Perry hadn't realized how long he'd sat at the table. Time was racing by, and he was still clothed in his pajamas, having not eaten yet nor used the bathroom. He stood from the table and considered calling the hospital. He'd do that, then get dressed and head down there.

He reached for the kitchen phone affixed to the wall chest-high but stopped when he heard a strange buzzing sound.

What the hell's that?

His hand neared the phone again, and the buzzing sound returned.

The clock on the stove said it was noon now.

Wait, that's impossible. How could an hour have sailed by while his only action was to stand from the chair and try to pick up the phone?

Something strange was happening. Was someone watching him? His normal aches and pains had disappeared, and time wasn't cooperating.

Some kind of trick was being played on him. Never one to be a victim (except with Marge), he lifted his leg high and strode from the kitchen, intent on his bedroom closet, getting regular clothes on, and then heading to the hospital.

When he entered the hallway, someone was crying upstairs. He ascended two stairs at a time and then listened to reassess where the crying was coming from.

It was his bedroom, his wife weeping, and the rustle of a dresser drawer closing.

When did she get home? How could he have missed her?

Oddly bemused at the eccentricity of this day so far but happy she was home and not in the hospital, he found himself perplexed even more.

He rushed through the door and entered their bedroom.

Marge didn't turn to acknowledge him. She just continued putting away her clothes and then sat on the edge of the bed to slip her legs into a pair of pants.

He waited for her to notice him. Once she was dressed and the rest of her clothes were placed away properly, Marge turned and looked directly at Perry.

He smiled, hoping she'd accept his apology.

She hugged herself, her eyes bloodshot from crying, her body language conveying weakness.

At that moment, Perry realized the damage he had caused with his explosive anger last night. But he'd had to tell her as their lives were in danger. He hadn't seen his son in fifteen years.

Previously, he'd decided that Marge didn't need to know about a man she would never meet, let alone have a relationship with. After Elton went to jail for life with no chance of parole for killing his mother and his two sisters, Perry packed up Marge and fled to Canada. Marge had never heard of Elton or Elton's mother because it was a mistake Perry didn't want to relive—ever.

When Perry and Marge had been married for ten years, Perry wondered if he'd made the right choice with his life. He was in his early forties and going through an internal crisis. He attended a conference in Las Vegas and slept with a stripper. It was the stupidest thing he had ever done. That stripper got pregnant. It just so happened that this particular peeler was religious enough to be pro-life. She had a baby boy named Elton and hunted down Perry. Although they'd only talked twice, she swore she would make sure their son would know who his father was and what he did.

Over the years, Perry never cheated again. He'd decided, since it was a one-night stand which he never intended to repeat, he simply wouldn't speak of it. He sent as much money as he could hide from Marge. He felt it was his duty, and every time he sent the money, he would apologize silently to Marge again and again, even though she had never known the truth.

Until last night.

Elton's mother raised him in a trailer outside Vegas near some commune. Elton killed her and his sisters at the age of twenty and went to prison. For reasons unknown to Perry, Elton was out of jail now and in Canada, too. Perry couldn't figure out how he got across the border as an ex-con, but he was here nonetheless and coming after his father.

Elton had been following him. He'd seen Elton standing across the street three times, watching the house.

So, he'd told Marge everything last night, and they'd fought.

As with anything in life, there are consequences for the actions taken. Now, he was about to receive his through the pain in her eyes.

He gestured toward her. "Marge, I'm sorry—"

"Perry, oh, Perry," she said, stumbling forward.

He watched her go past him and into the hallway. Perry took a deep breath and followed. He would have to work hard to make his peace with her.

He would have to let her deal with this any way she saw fit because she didn't deserve to be walloped in the cheek with the business end of a broom.

But then he needed to convince her to pack up and move to a hotel. Elton knew where they lived. He'd be back, and he would kill them the next time.

Perry followed her to the stairs. As he reached the bottom, he heard a faint clicking sound with each step. He looked down at the black dress shoes on his feet, then touched the suit jacket and shirt on his shoulders.

He was losing his mind. That had to be it. There was no way he could have gotten dressed without knowing about it, especially not in clothes he didn't even own. He could dismiss the extremely fast clock in the kitchen as dementia or find some illusory answer on why he was experiencing wonderful health. He could get checked for a brain tumor or something else of wild importance. But suddenly, being dressed for the Royal Ball in clothes he'd never seen before was something else entirely.

He scoured the downstairs and found Marge in the

reading room. She had a newspaper raised in front of her face. He took it as a cue to keep his distance. The chair in the corner by the phone table was his usual spot.

While waiting for Marge to come around, he might phone the police to let them know he'd seen Elton watching the house. Marge would hear his voice, and she'd be able to hear what he was saying to the police about how dangerous Elton was. Maybe she would put their safety over her anger and talk to him. It would also make her acknowledge his presence and remind her that the man she married forty-five years ago was still in the room. The man who'd made one mistake and was willing to pay any price for it.

Perry reached for the phone. His fingers were rewarded with dead air and that familiar buzzing sound from earlier in the kitchen. He looked directly at it and tried to lift it again but failed.

The phone rang at that moment. He jumped. Marge dropped her newspaper on the coffee table, stood, and approached him, bending to pick up the receiver.

"Hello?"

Marge paused and said hello again, only to frown and slowly set the phone down. Perry watched as she walked across the room to the kitchen without looking at him. He might as well be dead for all she was noticing him. Bewildered about how he couldn't pick up the phone, Perry sat and stared at it. He idly wondered if he was responsible for making it ring.

Marge worked away in the kitchen, making what he thought would be tea. He had to try to understand what was happening. He couldn't believe that Marge chose to avoid him by refusing to acknowledge his presence. She would not carry it on this long without even one look in his eyes. That fact startled him immensely.

And when did I get dressed? Where did I get these clothes from? How can I make the phone ring?

He stood and paced the floor. Voices called to him from a distance. It sounded like twenty or thirty people repeating his name in unison. It was like an echo in a narrow hallway when it reached his ears.

What the hell is that?

He looked around the living room but couldn't determine where the voices came from.

He stopped pacing and stared down at the newspaper Marge had been reading. It sat open on the coffee table. He saw a photo of a younger version of himself, dressed in black shoes and black suit pants, wearing the same jacket and shirt he wore now. He swung around the table and planted himself hard on the sofa, intent on finding out why he was in the newspaper.

The obituaries section featured an article dedicated to the memory of Marge's beloved husband, Perry Strall. Deceased four days ago. He was shot in the head in his home by an unknown assailant.

Perry stopped reading and touched his head. Everything was intact. He ran his hands all over his body. Nothing wrong. He felt an intense calling to warn Marge. He didn't know how he was still here or why. All he gathered was there must be a reason because he didn't *feel* dead. If he was dead, then it must be that he came back to warn Marge. That had to be the reason.

He read that his funeral had been the day the newspaper was printed, between eleven a.m. and noon. That might have something to do with why he lost track of time in the kitchen earlier.

The voices he'd been hearing increased in volume. Deep inside the intuitive area of his soul, Perry knew the newspaper article was not a cruel joke orchestrated by Marge to remind him of his own mortality.

He headed for the kitchen, intent on finding a way to talk to Marge. If he was still hanging around her, there must be a reason.

She sat at the kitchen table, eyes swollen, her lower lip quivering, stirring a cup of tea, a tissue in her hand. He glimpsed the kitchen phone. As he reached for it, the phones throughout the house began ringing. Marge looked up, stopped stirring the tea, and picked up the phone.

"Hello?" she said.

Perry spoke tentatively at first, not sure what to expect.

"Marge ..." he stopped as he saw a visible change over Marge's features. The lines on her face contorted as an intense weeping began. He also stopped because the voices—definitely calling him from somewhere in the house—sounded like they came from the next room.

"Perry?" Marge managed to wheeze out, gasping through tears.

"I'm here," he said, waiting for her to collect herself. "I wanted to apologize for hitting you. During our fight, emotions got out of control. I accidentally bumped the broom when I spun around to walk out of the kitchen. I'm sorry it hit your face."

She almost dropped the phone as her eyes widened. She completely ignored his apology. "What's happening, Perry? Are you … alive? Where are you?" She used the tissue to wipe her nose and eyes.

"I'm right beside you and here to warn you about Elton. He shot me. I'm sure of it." He turned around and looked behind him. The voices were really close. "They're calling me quite loudly just now. I think I have to go, honey."

"Oh, Perry, talk a little longer. Please stay, my love."

"I'm so sorry, Marge. I thought we'd be safe from Elton. I miscalculated. Please forgive—"

The doorbell rang.

Marge looked through the kitchen door and down the hallway.

"Don't answer it," he shouted. "You have to leave the house immediately."

"What's that? I have to what?"

Perry shouted with all the pent-up anger and emotion he could muster. "Run! Get out of the house. Get out now. Hurry —"

The doorbell rang again, cutting him off.

One of the voices spoke to Perry from right behind him, but he ignored the sound. He watched Marge and waited to see what she would do. Another noise came from the back of the house.

It startled Marge so much that she dropped the phone.

The connection was lost.

The loud crash of glass breaking emanated from the back of the house.

When Perry turned around, he gasped as his gaze fell

upon his mother. She'd passed away over thirty years before, but yet here she stood, radiant with a smile like a sun, hand held out to him, beckoning.

"Mother?"

"You can't help her now," she whispered, her mouth not moving. "You've done the best you could. It's time to come with us."

Perry stepped back. "No. My Marge is in trouble. She needs me. This is my fault. I intend to stop Elton."

"You can't, Perry. You've passed. You're on the other side now. Come with us."

"No!" he shouted. Nothing was going to make him leave Marge's side. Picture frames on the kitchen wall vibrated when he shouted.

His mother disappeared in a wisp of smoke. The voices that had crept up on him ceased their cacophony.

Perry turned around.

Marge was gone.

He ran through the hall and into the reading room. It was empty.

"Marge," he called out before realizing she couldn't hear him without the benefit of the phone. He ran down the hall toward the back of the house. The mud room window by the washing machine was completely broken out. Glass littered the small brown mat.

He called out again, even though it was fruitless.

A thumping noise came from the cellar.

He bolted for the basement door and down the stairs as if he floated. Elton was there, his back to Perry. Marge was in the corner, down on her knees.

"Why are you doing this?" she asked.

"Because I have a father who left me to die. I believe in divine justice."

"You think what you did to my husband was divine justice?"

Elton kicked out the step ladder's legs and sat on the top step. Perry walked around in front of his son. One of Perry's drills rested in his hand.

"Okay, we have a little time," Elton said. "I'll explain. My mother was a whore. Do you know how many men she would bring home? They would beat me for fun. I lost my fingerprints at the age of eight because one of the men my mother brought home didn't want people to be able to identify me. How did he know I'd live a life of crime?" Elton held his free hand up and showed Marge his fingers. "He burned them off on the kitchen stove while my mother laughed at me. She also said dental records help to identify people, so they never took me to a dentist. I lost almost all my teeth and never had the money for those fake ones until I was in jail. The system paid for it. See." Elton opened his mouth displaying a white band of teeth in a wide smile.

"I'm sorry. I'm so terribly sorry," Marge said. "No one should have to live under those conditions."

"Got my high school diploma in prison."

"Are you doing this to hurt the people that hurt you?"

"Something like that."

Marge wiped her eyes.

Elton continued, "Your husband, my father, left me with that woman, who DNA calls my mother. She had two other girls that were beaten and raped more times than I know how to count. They were really twisted. I'm the only sane one to walk out of that house from Hell. I killed them all to end their pain. My one sister thanked me on her last breath as the night before. Three men anally raped her while our mother collected the cash. She even helped secure her daughter's hands. Well, now I've killed my dad for allowing that pain in the first place by not stepping up to the plate. You're the last one who has to die."

"Why me? I am not connected to what happened to you or your family."

"The rule for me goes like this." Elton massaged the drill like a pet cat sitting in his lap. "You hurt me. I hurt you back. You take something from me. I take something from you."

"I haven't taken anything from you."

Elton lifted his head back and moaned as he looked up at the basement's ceiling. "You people. Nobody gets it. Okay, I'll explain. My dad hurt me badly, so I hurt him. He took away my life. Now I take something from him, and that's you. Then everything will be right with the world."

Marge was losing control again. She sobbed heavier and bobbed her shoulders as her old body shuddered.

"I like seeing your fear," he whispered. "And you know what, I don't care about it. I'll tell you why. I lived in fear all of my life because of my father. He could've brought me here and raised me with you, but he didn't. Instead, I feared waking up every morning. Do you want to know the worst thing that happened to me?"

Marge shook her head back and forth. "No. I'm so sorry …"

"Shut up! I don't want your fucking pity. You're nothing

to me." He leaned back, still caressing the drill in his lap. "The worst thing was when I was ten. My mom was out whoring somewhere, and she had her current boyfriend babysitting me. I almost died that night. I was in the hospital for two weeks. I look back and still can't figure out what set him off. He was drinking, and then he was violent. He ripped off all my clothes and did things to me that were unspeakable. I bled in my shit for over a week. He knocked teeth out, broke three fingers, and almost cost me one of my eyes. And you know what my mother did? She said I probably deserved it. I was ten years fucking old, and already I wanted to murder people. That man died in some gang robbery two months later. I was so happy that I even thanked a God I didn't believe in. Crazy, huh?"

All Marge could do was whisper, "I'm so sorry."

Perry needed to do something, but he was rooted in the story. He would've done something years ago if he had known of this. He glanced around, but there was no phone in the basement.

The drill started up.

Marge screamed.

Perry watched in horror as Elton walked toward his wife of forty-five years. Perry screamed and shouted her name, but no one heard him.

Then he moved between them, but Elton walked through him.

If there was nothing he could do, then why was he here? Why torture him like this?

Perry moved up to Elton and screamed a violent torrent of rage.

Elton's hair lifted slightly. His son scanned the windows to see if they were open. Marge curled up in the corner, trying to get as far away from the drill as possible.

Perry screamed again, but this time, it had no effect.

Elton got down on one knee, grabbed Marge's hair, and tilted her head back, then rammed the drill's business end into her right eye.

Perry fell apart as his wife's body went through a series of convulsions.

Then he heard her say his name.

He spun around and saw Marge standing behind him. He did a double take and then looked back at her corpse on their basement floor.

"Marge?"

His mother showed up again.

Those voices entered his consciousness.

His mother spoke first. "Perry. We all have loved ones come for us when we pass over. I'm here for you. You're here for Marge."

He stared at Marge. She looked fabulous.

Then, the basement was gone. They were outside. He thought he'd lost rational thought. Nothing made sense. Was he even sane anymore after witnessing that macabre scene?

A gunshot resounded from inside the house.

"Elton will be joining us soon," his mother said. "Elton's pain is over now, too. Come. Join the rest of your family. We're all here to accept everyone."

Perry merged with his wife, and their souls held each other as they lifted away from the house where they'd spent their marriage.

The Uniqueness of Life

A COLD WIND BLEW Rebecca's hair up, her eyes closing as they watered. The street was mostly empty, except for two women entering the gift shop Rebecca had just left.

What gave her such a feeling of dread? Why did she feel like something was wrong?

A store window caught her attention. She slowed and stared at a wall of televisions. The different-sized screens were all tuned to the same news station, showing image after image of the current snowstorm blanketing the province just south of them. She shivered as the cold seemed to move right through her. The volume on the TVs was too low to catch what was being said through the store's window pane and the large earmuffs she wore, but she watched anyway, transfixed by the pictures on the screens. When she made to turn away, movement in the corner of the window stopped her. She did a double take.

It was the reflection of a man standing across the street, staring at her. Even through the reflection and the angle of the window, she was sure he was watching her.

It was her husband, Mark.

Rebecca spun around and looked across the road at her husband, many thoughts going through her mind. Why wasn't he at work? Was he following her? Why didn't he come over and say something?

"Mark," she yelled, waving her gloved hands.

He nodded and turned away.

"Mark!" she yelled again as he disappeared around the corner of a building.

What the hell was that about?

Rebecca ran as fast as she could manage on the slippery snow. She made it to the flashing yellow light on her side, and after looking up and down Main Street, she hustled across. In less than a minute, she'd reached the spot where Mark had been and then looked around the corner where he'd turned.

He was gone.

That was strange. Why would he take off like that?

She reached into her coat pocket and pulled out her cell phone. After dialing his office number, she got his voicemail. She tried his cell. No answer.

Okay, that's super strange.

The incident only intensified the butterflies in her stomach, confirming to herself something was wrong. Mark wouldn't just walk away like that, at least not after fifteen years of marriage. He was acting more like a stranger than her husband.

She decided to finish the banking she'd come here to do, then leave the downtown area. The cold had kept many people indoors today, but Mark had asked her to deposit at the bank for him. She'd thought she would add some shopping to her excursion, but now she just wanted to get home.

Besides, why did he ask her to do his banking when he was downtown, too? He could've just done it himself.

While more questions brewed in her thoughts, she made it to the bank without seeing him again. The front doors were large wooden ones that opened to two more doors that had been added for security. She stepped through and immediately headed for the line.

Only one teller worked the counter. Four people waited to be served, which meant at least five to ten minutes of standing around. She lined up anyway but kept a watchful eye on the window looking out at the street.

Random cars passed, their exhaust smoky in the cold January morning air. She reveled in the heat of the bank, loosening her scarf and removing her mittens. She pulled off her earmuffs and placed them in her oversized purse.

The line moved. Two people in front of her. After a minute, the line moved again.

When she faced the bank's window, Mark stood staring at her.

He was up against the glass, his nose touching it. It was a hard stare, like he was trying to bore through her, his face forward, forehead almost touching the pane, too.

She frowned and gestured with her hands, mouthing the

words, *what's going on?*

It was eerie how he seemed to be immobile. He looked like he was made of stone, and—although he wasn't dressed well enough for the weather—he didn't appear to be shivering.

The people ahead of her in the line moved forward. Rebecca was next now. The bank's doors opened, and a woman in her twenties walked over to stand behind Rebecca, removing her hat and blowing into her cupped palms.

Rebecca glanced back at her husband, confusion turning to anger.

Why didn't he come in out of the cold and wait with her? She was here for him, after all.

She waved for him to join her.

He touched the window, palm open. He waited a few seconds and then smacked the window.

Rebecca jumped. The woman behind her looked up.

"You okay?"

Rebecca pointed at her husband. "That didn't startle you? When he smacked the window?"

The young woman looked over at the bank's window and then back at Rebecca.

"Who smacked the window? What're you talking about?"

An eerie sensation coursed through her as if she were in a movie. None of this was real.

She looked back out at her husband again.

His hand came away from the glass, and he beckoned for her to join him.

Come outside, he motioned.

She frowned. Didn't he want her to finish the banking he asked her to do?

After a few seconds, he waved his hand faster, struggling to keep his head straight. He looked like he was having an epileptic seizure on the sidewalk.

Rebecca decided to step out of line and leave the bank.

"Fine, fuck it—do your own banking."

She placed the earmuffs back on her head, the gloves on her hands, and tightened her scarf. She had to put an end to this insanity. She could always come back in after talking to him or send him into his own shit.

She didn't want to acknowledge that the woman in line behind her couldn't see him—that was not something she was ready to accept.

She hit the inner doors and started through them as two burly men entered. It struck her as odd because they wore matching green long-sleeved turtlenecks with no coats.

One of the men knocked into her, causing Rebecca to stumble into the wall.

"Hey," she said, recovering her balance.

How could people be so rude?

They ignored her and continued into the bank, shutting the doors behind them. An audible click sounded as the thumb lock snapped in place.

Why would they lock the doors?

She headed for the outside with bigger questions on her mind.

The cold hit her immediately. She hopped down the few steps, being mindful of any ice buildup, and spun around the edge of the building to face Mark.

The sidewalk was empty.

He had vanished again.

Her eyes had been off him no more than five seconds.

It was impossible, but he'd vanished—again.

It was not only ridiculous. It was getting stupid because now she was pissed off.

The comment by the woman in the bank, suggesting that she hadn't been able to see Mark at the window, returned to her.

She shook it off and moved to stand where her husband had stood not half a minute before.

Firecrackers sounded from inside the bank.

Then someone screamed.

What she saw through the bank window chilled her more than the icy cold that tried to permeate her clothing.

The two men in green turtleneck sweaters who had brushed past her in the doorway were holding guns. The woman standing in line behind her was crouched on her knees on the cold floor.

One of the gunmen grabbed the woman's hair and shouted something. Rebecca heard the woman scream. The man placed a weapon against the woman's head. The other gunman was trying to convince the teller to do something.

Then, the gun exploded in the gunman's hand. The woman's hair puffed up on the opposite side of her head, her eyes opening wide as she crumpled to the floor.

Without realizing she was doing it or the danger involved, Rebecca screamed. The gunman turned and looked at her. He swiveled his gun in her direction.

She tried to run but slipped on the snow and fell. The

second she made contact with the snow-covered sidewalk, the glass above her shattered as bullets broke through it.

Rebecca crawled on the frozen ground. She cleared the base of the window, got to her feet, and ran three steps to the edge of the building, where she turned behind the brick wall and dove for the snow bank the plow had left after cleaning the parking lot.

No bullets followed her.

Fearful they would give chase, Rebecca got to her feet and headed for the alleyway behind the bank, where she hopped a fence to disappear down the street on another block.

A police siren wailed in the distance.

Why had she stood and watched that woman die? Why didn't she grab her phone or bang on the bank's windows?

When her cell phone rang, she jumped and almost slipped again.

In a panic, she grabbed at her phone.

"Hello?" Her voice sounded hesitant, broken.

"My name is Doctor Manning. I'm on staff at Liberty Memorial. I would like to speak with Rebecca Saffren, please."

"This is, I mean, I'm Rebecca."

The cold had seeped back in. Her body was now performing a whole-body shiver.

"I'm sorry to tell you this over the phone, but your husband has been in an accident."

"What? Is he all right?" Then, another thought occurred to her. "He's not dead, is he?" She slowed down, turned a corner, and continued walking quicker, her joints stiffening with the cold as she moved. Her left knee had taken most of the fall in front of the bank. It ached enough to make her limp now.

"Oh no, he's not dead. We wouldn't tell you something like that over the phone, Mrs. Saffren. He came in four hours ago. He was in a car accident this morning. Your husband's a lucky man. His injuries aren't that bad, considering what happened to the car. His right arm is broken, and he suffered a good-sized hit on the head. He's been unconscious since we brought him in. Only two minutes ago, he woke up and told us he wanted to speak to you. He supplied your cell number since it wasn't with his identification. He's asking if you could come to the hospital. It's strange, though."

She stopped and leaned against the building beside her, trying to catch her breath, shivering more than she thought was possible. "What's, str … strange?"

"He said he needs to know if you have left the bank yet. I'm not sure what that means."

The sirens in the distance were much closer.

She told the doctor she was on her way and shut her phone.

Rebecca rushed to her car, convinced Mark had saved her life somehow. She still couldn't account for how she'd seen him in the street if he'd been in the hospital all morning, but deep down inside, she knew he had come for her.

Somehow, he showed up.

It was her turn to show up for him.

***

Parking at the hospital proved easy to find. She had found the drive over calming, with the heater on full, alone with her thoughts. There was a moment on the way when she thought she'd have to pull over to throw up, but she was able to resist it. She'd never seen anyone killed before, nor was she even sure that it happened.

What was real and what wasn't?

Rebecca entered the hospital by the emergency doors and —after asking for her husband—was given directions.

Five minutes of meandering through the labyrinthine halls of the medical building brought her to a ward where she found Mark sitting up in bed behind a curtained-off area.

She took in his injuries, the cast on his broken arm.

"Oh, Mark." She moved closer and kissed his forehead. "What happened?"

He blinked and looked up at her, his eyes watering. "I had this dream. I saw you in the bank." His eyes searched her face frantically. "I thought you'd be killed or something. Like I felt it in my soul. I wanted you out of that bank so bad that I bet everything I owned on persuading you to join me on my side of the window where you'd be safe. Does any of that make sense?"

Rebecca wiped at the tears that now clouded her vision. All the calm she had gathered on the way to the hospital was lost.

She realized she hadn't taken off her gloves yet. She removed them, loosened her scarf, and yanked her earmuffs off backward so they could rest on her neck.

Two beds down, a commotion was taking place, but neither could see what was happening as the curtains blocked their view.

"I saw the whole thing," she said. "It was horrible."

"What did you see?" Mark asked as he used his good hand to wipe her face.

"These men entered the bank and …" Rebecca broke down.

Since seeing Mark in the street and then being shot at, her nerves were frayed. Now safe in his arms, she fell apart.

He held her as best he could with his one unbroken arm.

"It's okay, let it out. You're safe now. You're with me. It's okay."

The disturbance grew in volume coming from the right side. The curtain was bumped a few times as doctors attempted to work on what sounded like an unruly patient.

Rebecca opened her purse and pulled out a Kleenex. She blew her nose and wiped at her eyes. After taking a deep, calming breath, she started talking again.

She explained how she saw him in the street and followed him. Then he was at the bank's window, and it was strange that the woman beside her in line couldn't see him. She had to pause at the part where the woman was shot in front of her and how it would've been her if she had remained in the bank.

Mark could tell there was more, so he prompted her.

Rebecca looked him in the eye, then told him how they shot at her through the bank window and how she fell by accident, which probably saved her life. Moments after getting away from the area, the hospital called her.

"And that's it," she said.

"I don't know what happened or why," Mark said.

"Everything you describe, I saw in my head. I didn't know I was here until I woke and asked them to call you. I needed to know if you made it out in time."

"I did, Mark, I did. Thanks to you."

The commotion next door grew in intensity. A man yelled at the doctor to get out of his face.

"Move aside!" the man shouted.

Rebecca stared at Mark and then at the curtain separating their small areas.

Fingers wrapped around the edge of the curtain.

Before she knew what was happening, the curtain was yanked back violently, and she was looking into the face of the bank robber who'd shot the woman in line.

He stared at them, smiling at Rebecca.

"Your cell phone rang, did it?" he asked, almost breathing the words through his teeth.

Rebecca gasped and clamped a hand over her mouth.

He lifted his head off his pillow and tried to stand but stopped halfway, the pain evident on his face.

"I was trying to do my banking," he continued. "I'm an innocent bystander. I was shot in the leg. Although," he looked around, and comfortable that no one could hear him, he continued, "you are the only person who could fuck with my story. That means we have a problem. What are you going to do? What am I going to do?"

He smiled, even though Rebecca could see the pain caused him great discomfort.

Mark looked up at Rebecca and then back at the wounded bank robber.

"She's going to tell the police what she saw, and you will

spend a considerable time in prison thinking about how fucked you are ..."

Rebecca cut him off. "Mark, no. I think we're in a unique position to help this man. By doing so, we can help each other."

Mark turned so fast to look at her that he grunted. "Shit, that hurt. What are you talking about?"

"Trust me," Rebecca said, not taking her eyes off the bank robber.

He smiled from his bed and leaned his head back down. "I'm happy you can see things my way."

"What are you doing?" Mark asked.

She let go of her husband and started around his bed. For a brief second, she vanished past the curtain and appeared again on the bank robber's side.

"Tell us what to do. We don't want trouble."

"That's what I was banking on. Ha, get it?" He paused to look between them. Lowering his voice, he said, "Forget it. Look, I won't threaten to kill you or say that I can use your hospital chart to get your name or any of that stuff. I won't go into how easy it would be to silence this little problem I now have. No, I won't do any of that. I want to be polite. I would like to ask that you give your word that you won't say or do anything to harm me, and I won't harm you. We go our separate ways. Deal?"

"Deal."

A doctor was pushed past her by a man in a security uniform.

"This man wasn't allowing me to stitch his leg," the doctor said. "He needs to be restrained, or I will have to sedate him." The doctor stopped and looked at the patient. "I don't want to have someone forcibly hold you down after what you've been through, and the police asked me not to sedate you as they want a statement when I'm done. So, will you allow me to finish?"

The bank robber looked from the security guard to Rebecca and then to the doctor. He nodded. "Go ahead. Get it done so I can give my statement and go home."

Rebecca stepped back and nodded at him, moving her fingers across her lips in a mum's-the-word gesture.

Then she disappeared around the corner.

On the first floor, she found two police officers having coffee.

"Are you two waiting for the man from the bank robbery?"

The one with the seventies mustache looked up at her. "Why would that matter to you?"

"I was there."

He looked at his partner and then back up to Rebecca. "You were there?"

"Yes. I saw that woman who was shot in the head. That man lying in the bed upstairs with a bullet wound to the leg did it."

The cop looked her up and down. He set his coffee on the table and stood, making Rebecca step back. His partner stood, too.

"Is that right? What else can you tell us?"

The cop was on the defensive. She could tell by his body language. He was ready to pounce, and she had no idea why.

"I was waiting in line, and it was taking too long," she

started, knowing she couldn't add anything remotely close to the truth. There was no way they'd believe her story of Mark saving her life. "I decided I couldn't wait any longer and headed outside just as the two burly men entered the bank. I was lucky enough to get out when I did. I heard something going on inside the bank and turned in time to see a man shoot a girl in the head. Then he saw me watching him and shot at me through the window. I fell into the snow and then got up and ran away. I came here because my husband was in a car accident, which is unrelated."

The cop crossed his arms. "There's a few things that are confusing me."

Rebecca frowned. "What's that?"

"First, you say you couldn't wait that long in line. The girl who was killed was the only one in line, according to the teller. You say there were two robbers. We only have one dead robber still at the bank. A witness a block down said he saw a woman matching your description jumping some kind of fence and running down another street away from the bank. The guy upstairs says there was another robber. He said it was a woman. She has the same hair and coat you're wearing. Can you explain any of that?"

While he was talking, his partner had placed his hand on the butt of his sidearm.

"What are you saying?" she stammered. "You think I'm involved somehow? That's ridiculous. I ran for my life. That guy upstairs shot at me. I almost died. My husband saved my life." Her exasperation was showing. She couldn't help it.

"Your husband saved your life? How could he do that? You said he was here after having a car accident. You used the word, '*unrelated.*'"

The cop stepped forward.

"Wait, you're not listening. You don't understand … no, wait."

The partner had stepped behind her and pulled her hands behind her back. Then handcuffs were slapped on her.

"Wait, this is all wrong." She tried to turn around, but they kept her facing the other way.

"You have the right to remain silent. You have the right to an attorney—"

"Wait!" she shouted. "I didn't do anything." She stopped when she saw Mark. He was standing ten feet behind them, smiling.

Rebecca felt the cop follow her gaze. She was sure he saw nothing because he looked back at her, confused.

Mark motioned for her to bend over. She frowned. He motioned again, but this time, he showed her, bending at the waist. When he stood up, he raised three fingers. Slowly, he lowered the first. Then he lowered the second.

The cops moved her. They said something about taking her downtown to tell her story. She caught a glimpse of Mark dropping his third finger.

Rebecca ducked, bucking her body hard.

A gunshot rang out. The cop to her right dropped to the ground, blood leaving his head wound as fast as a fountain.

A siren sounded throughout the hospital.

Another gunshot and the other officer dropped just as fast, blood oozing from his left cheekbone where a bullet hole ruined his staunch features.

"I knew you'd tell the first cops you encountered."

The criminal limped with the use of a crutch. A large white bandage was wrapped around his thigh, and his pant legs were cut to just above the wound.

"You couldn't help yourself, could you?"

Rebecca edged closer to the police officer lying dead beside her. She needed to get to his gun, even though she'd never used one in her life.

"What did you do to my husband?"

"He's dead. Are you fucking stupid? I couldn't walk away with you two knowing my secret. I'll still walk away from this, but the death toll will be higher. Although that's not my fault—it's yours."

He lifted his weapon. The hospital alarm blared. Rebecca eased the last few inches over and blindly felt the cop's holster, her fingers feeling desperate for the butt of the weapon.

Someone had screamed when the cop fell, and others ran.

Where was everybody? Was she going to die on the floor here, handcuffed like she was?

Her hands wrapped around the gun.

The bank robber's weapon hadn't fired by the time she pulled out the cop's weapon.

She rolled onto her stomach and hoped her aim was true.

The bank robber stood six feet from her, his weapon aimed at her face.

The hospital siren wailed on. A nurse entered the area where they were and screamed. She ran back through the door she had just come through.

The bank robber's gun fired as Rebecca fumbled with the cop's weapon, trying to get it right in her hand without looking.

Her finger found the trigger and began squeezing it. After several pulls, the weapon dropped from her hands, and her body went into some kind of seizure.

The bank robber's bullet had entered the back of her head.

***

Rebecca's eyes opened.

She tried to get up but was restrained by the pain. The last thoughts she'd had came back to her.

A metal stand was beside her, pumping something into her arm. Some kind of cloth covered her neck and head. Feeling around with her free hand, she discovered bandages.

A machine beeped beside her, increasing in tempo with her heartbeat.

A door opened. She tried to look toward it, but more pain welcomed that movement.

"You're awake."

The doctor who had attended the bank robber stood over her, looking down with a silly smile under his thick glasses.

"What happened?" she asked, her mouth feeling like it was packed with sand.

The doctor turned away and returned with a glass of water, a bendable straw sticking out of it. She drank greedily until he pulled it from her.

"A lot has happened. You were shot by the guy who killed two police officers."

"What happened to him?" Rebecca asked, her stomach

churning as it all came back to her.

"He's dead now. He didn't make it out of the parking lot. The investigation took weeks, but they pieced it all together. I was told you were at the bank, and we told the police what your husband said about calling you. They haven't figured out that part yet, but at least they know you weren't part of it." He stopped, looked down at her, and raised one thumb. "That was some crazy gun use you did. Shot the robber in the stomach, dead center. He stumbled out of the hospital and collapsed in the parking lot, where he died under police gunfire. They found a memory stick on him with the schematics of the bank. It was in all the newspapers as far away as Toronto. They're calling you a hero."

It was too much to take in. She was happy he was dead but needed to know about Mark.

"What happened to my husband?"

He looked away. "I'm sorry. You've been out for almost a month now. Your head wound was severe. We were worried you would wake up and not remember anything or not wake at all."

"My husband," Rebecca cut him off.

"He died. The bank job guy strangled him in his bed after you went downstairs that fateful day."

Rebecca cried. After a moment, the doctor stepped away. Then she heard the door open and close.

She cried because even in death, he had come for her. She wept because he'd saved her life again when he got her to duck.

Rebecca whispered goodbye to her husband. "I'll see you in my dreams, my eternal love."

Stuck

Stan Rickstead's alarm sounded. He entered the dark and fumbled with the switch, but the alarm continued.

It was his pager going off. He grabbed it and lit up the screen.

The most dreaded words in his profession scrolled there: *emerg-911. Call HQ en route.*

For calls such as these, he stayed prepared. His uniform was laid out, gun cleaned, boots shined, lunch already made and sitting in their second fridge in the garage. Lydia always had his lunch ready before she went to her night shift at the 24-hour Excite Drug Mart. She'd never forgotten to make his lunch in the fifteen years they'd been married.

Minutes later, Stan was running for the door to the garage, thinking about how much he loved his wife and all the little things she did for him. They were conscious of how rare their marriage was because everything clicked, everything worked, and they never fought. Love was a puzzle, one that most people had trouble figuring out. But for Stan and Lydia, their pieces fell together with little effort.

He fired up his pickup, backed out of the garage, and slammed the accelerator down. The clock on the dash told him it was just after four in the morning, which meant there wouldn't be anybody on the road to get in his way.

He unclipped the cell phone from its cradle on the dash and dialed headquarters. It was picked up on the second ring.

"Wallace Pine Police."

"Nancy, it's Stan. I received a page about an emergency situation. What can you tell me?"

"It's not good. Jake and the boys are down there."

"Down where?"

"This whacko has already shot two people, and he's got three hostages: a woman and two men. Jake asked me to page you so you could go down and try to talk to the guy. He needs your negotiating skills."

"What happened to the two people the perp shot?"

"He let them go so we could get them to the hospital. They're over at Lindsay Memorial right now, already headed into surgery."

"Okay, I'm on my way, but you need to tell me where I'm going."

"The all-night drug store. You know the one, Excite Drug Mart."

Stan tuned her out. He lowered the phone from his ear and set it on the seat beside him.

Lydia worked there—the night shift. Could Lydia be the

female hostage?

I'm in a dream. This can't be happening.

He brought the phone to his ear again as his foot pressed harder on the accelerator.

"Nancy, you still there?"

"Yes."

"The two people who were injured, was one female?"

"No, both male. Is everything okay, Stan?"

"Tell me about the hostages," he said, spittle crossing his lips, teeth tight together.

"There's one woman—we think she's an employee—and two males, unidentified as of this moment."

"Tell Jake I'm minutes away."

He raced through the downtown area of Wallace Pine at a reckless pace. He had no experience in negotiating for a loved one. All his precedents were with strangers. Not to say they were of any less value, only emotions weren't attached to them. This would be personal, which meant he had no idea how it would play out. Everything he'd say or do could be tainted.

Knowing all that, though, he wanted it no other way. If anyone would get Lydia out safely, it had to be him.

Up ahead, the lights of the patrol cars flashed off building walls. Wallace Pine had three cruisers, and they were all present.

Stan pulled in behind Jake's cruiser, exited, then ducked around back, where he met up with Jake and two of his men.

"What's happening?"

"The guy's got three hostages. No demands yet. He's tied up the two males. The woman goes with him whenever he moves from aisle to aisle."

"Is he strapped?"

"Yes. It looks like a Glock, but we can't confirm that."

"Do I have a direct line?"

"Right over there." Jake pointed to an office building, kitty corner with the drug store. "Mark is in there by the phone. Everything is set for you. And hey, Stan, doesn't Lydia work here?"

"Yes, the night shift." His voice trailed off as he looked at the drug store windows.

"Good luck, Stan. Everyone goes home alive tonight, okay."

Jake patted Stan's shoulder, and then Stan ran to the office building. The phone sat on a table by the main front window. A pad of paper and pen sat beside it. Stan lifted the phone and hit the speed dial button beside the words, *Excite Drug Mart*. It was picked up on the third ring.

"Hello, this is Stan Rickstead. Is there anything I can get you?"

"Yeah," a male voice answered.

"What do you need? Transportation?" Stan tried to keep his voice calm, level. The man he was talking to had his Lydia. He also had a gun and was willing to use it as he'd already shot people.

"I need a new life. This one doesn't work so well."

"We can help with things like that. We've got qualified people who can help. But first, we need to end this predicament we're in." Stan brushed sweat from his brow. He realized how nervous he was when he saw his hand shaking.

He looked across the street. There was no visible

movement in the drugstore.

"I just came in for a few prescriptions, and these two guys tried to give me a hard time, saying my slips were fakes. I'm sorry I hurt them. I didn't want to hurt nobody."

"I understand. Why don't you put your gun down and come on outside? We can figure everything out." Stan's hand ached at the joints, but he wasn't releasing his grip on the phone.

"No, I'm done talking. Don't call again. I won't answer."

The line died.

Stan couldn't sit there and do nothing. Lydia needed him. He had to get her out.

Stan exited the office building and made his way to the back of the drug store on the opposite side of where Jake and his men were waiting behind their cruisers. A lone officer was watching the back door. Stan nodded to him and pulled out his keys. Lydia and Stan had identical key rings in the event one of them locked themselves out. On Stan's ring was a key to Excite's back door.

He unlocked the door slowly and eased it open. Darkness swallowed him as he entered the stock room. He walked through the small back room and made his way up the cough medicine aisle undetected. The aim was to come in behind where the perp was last seen through the window.

Then Stan saw his wife.

She stumbled into the aisle five feet from him, alone.

Where's the perp?

A red stain had formed on Lydia's shirt in the stomach area.

His wife had been shot.

He gasped audibly.

Lydia turned away and stumbled into a rack of cough syrup. She hit the ground hard. Stan was close enough to see her eyes roll back in her head.

The pain he felt for not being there quicker was too much to handle. He had not been able to save his wife. He couldn't protect her.

Staring at Lydia, mesmerized by her, he missed movement to his right.

Stan spun and ducked, his weapon raised.

A gun fired.

***

Stan Rickstead's alarm sounded. He entered the dark and fumbled with the switch, but the alarm continued.

It was his pager going off. He grabbed it and lit up the screen.

The most dreaded words in his profession scrolled there: emerg-911. Call HQ en route.

For calls such as these, he stayed prepared. His uniform was laid out, gun cleaned, boots shined, lunch already made and sitting in their second fridge in the garage. Lydia always had his lunch ready before she went to her night shift at the 24-hour Excite Drug Mart. She'd never forgotten to make his lunch in the fifteen years they'd been married.

Maybe this time, he'd save her.

If he didn't, he'd try again. And again. And again.

***

Lydia stared at her empty garage. It had been two years since the hostage-taking at the drug mart. Two years since she had lost her husband.

She wished she could return it and not go to work that night. Not try to help the two wounded men. She had had a chance to run for the exit—she could have actually made it out of the building. But she stayed to make sure everyone was okay. She thought she could handle it.

She had seen the look on her husband's face. He'd seen the blood on her shirt. What Stan didn't know was the blood belonged to the wounded men she had helped. It wasn't her blood.

She had fainted and fell into the cough syrup stand as the shock, exhaustion, and fatigue caught up with her. No doubt Stan thought she had been shot. There could be no other reason for him to turn on the guy and fire. And, of course, there was return fire. Stan had grazed the guy. The criminal's aim had been better, with his first bullet going through Stan's heart.

Lydia looked at her watch: 4:10 a.m. Right on time. Ever since Stan's funeral, Lydia heard the sound of his pager going off. It happened every morning at 4:00 a.m. A distant sound, like it was coming from somewhere else. She also heard noises in the garage. Then, the garage door would open and close all on its own.

Every morning at 4:06 a.m.

She wondered if it was Stan, reliving that night over and over in a vain attempt to save her.

She sure hoped not. What a hell that would be. Trapped

by such an intense love.

She shook her head and went back upstairs to bed.

An Illusion of Haunting

I AM THE HAUNTER, the haunted, and the haunting.

I can't believe what I just witnessed. My heart is pumping in my chest like it's trying to escape. I have to gulp air to keep it in. I'm so nervous my hands can hardly manipulate the wheels of my wheelchair. But I have to move because I must tell somebody what I've just seen. Someone has to know. I mean, this isn't real, is it?

I turned from the window. It took me a full minute to exit the guest bedroom. This doorway hadn't been renovated after the car accident six years ago when my wife died. I thought I'd never use this room again, so why waste money renovating it?

This was the first time I'd rolled into it in over three months. I'm wondering why I did it in the first place.

The image of what I'd just seen rolled over and over in

my head like the film on a projector, casting a horrid scene in my brain that I could not banish.

My house is two stories high. The money from my wife's life insurance policy enabled me to have the chair lift for the stairs installed in the house and access ramps added, along with other modifications.

I loaded myself onto the elevator and started my descent. Halfway down, I remembered there was a phone in my bedroom.

What's wrong with me? Why am I not thinking more clearly?

I would've missed it if what I'd just witnessed happened seconds earlier or later. There has to be a reason I saw the accident. There just has to be. I believe in omens and premonitions. I had been chosen to witness it—me alone.

Captain Michaels runs the town like it's his own. This kind of thing never happens in our quiet little town of Michael's Bay—the captain has no connection to the town's name.

When I got downstairs, I rolled out of the lift and went to the phone in the living room. I hit speed dial and selected the hands-free feature. After the proper amount of rings, Captain Michaels himself answered the phone.

"Frank. It's Bryce Montgomery. I just witnessed a car accident."

Why am I running out of breath when I'm just sitting?

"Calm down, Bry. Start at the beginning. Where are you right now?"

"At home. In my living room." I stopped and gulped in air like I was eating it now. Maybe I was having a heart attack, and the pain would come next. I tried to ooze lower into my chair, looking for a calmer, more relaxed position. "From my guest-room window, I just witnessed an older model white Honda Prelude hit a guy. He's still lying in the street."

"Did you say you saw this from your guest room window?"

Why would he ask that? A man is dying in the street.

Captain Michaels has been inside my house numerous times. Before she died, he'd visited my wife and me for Christmas and Thanksgiving more times than I can count. Captain Michaels and I were close in high school, and he was the best man at my wedding.

My wife Virginia always tried to set him up with one of her girlfriends. After many years, we'd learned to get used to the idea that the captain had married his job.

"There's a man lying in the street in front of my house. He could very well be dead, and you're asking me what room I was in? You know my guest room faces the street."

"Well, Bry, you haven't been in your guest room for almost three months."

This was the second time Frank Michaels surprised me with a weird comment. Maybe the captain had been drinking and didn't understand what I was saying.

Wait, drinking? Why would I think that? What's going on with me? And how did he know how often I visited this or that room?

"Do you understand what I've told you?" I asked. I scanned the room, feeling watched now.

"Of course, I understand. I'll be right over. You watch

how quick I'll be. Just hang on. Wait for me, okay, Bry? Don't go outside without me." The line died.

Why was he calling me Bry instead of Bryce? Virginia was the only one who ever called me Bry. I hadn't heard that in a long time.

The car accident that took her life wasn't my fault. I know I was driving, but the accident wasn't my fault. I keep telling myself that, but it doesn't work. The truth is, Virginia, the love of my life, died on that snowy highway Christmas evening, 2006, because of me. No one else was behind the wheel. I lost both legs above the knee.

I glanced back at my front door. It was shut, and it was locked from where I was sitting—the thumb bolt turned horizontal.

"What the hell's going on?"

No one answered me.

I must be daydreaming, thinking about Virginia again. There hadn't been a day since the accident that I didn't think about that night, about my wife. Could I have done something different when I saw the headlights veer toward us? Could I have turned right instead of turning to the left and exposing the passenger side to the oncoming car?

Not now, I said to myself. Snap out of it. The captain is on his way. Probably an ambulance or coroner, too. That guy was whacked pretty hard. Wonder what he was doing in the street in the first place.

Something scratched the wood flooring upstairs. I looked up but only saw the ceiling of the living room. I heard a thump, and then what I can only describe as something heavy was dragged along the floor.

Someone was in the house.

I picked up the phone again. The line was dead. No dial tone.

What are they after? Who are they? I have nothing of value. The insurance money is gone now. Disability paychecks are small. Only an idiot would try to rob me.

I'm not the best in physical situations, as I'm bound to a chair with moveable parts, so I rolled to the front door, unlocked and opened it, then bounced my wheels onto the front porch.

People across the street had gathered. I counted twelve so far. I looked up and down the street but saw no sign of the white Honda Prelude.

I eased out farther and spun my chair around to look up at the second-story windows. Nothing looked wrong. No one stood there, looking down at me.

Michaels's siren wailed in the distance. I rolled out to the sidewalk. I was safe outside. Whoever was in my house would be in serious shit as soon as the cops arrived.

As I waited, I took in the sweet smell of summer. The heat rose toward midday. This was Virginia's favorite time of year. She loved early May. It was time to work in her garden and clean the windows. She used to say she cleaned them to remove the touch that a cold winter would leave behind. I never understood that, but I do now, as I've been touched by the cold hand I was dealt. Bound in a wheelchair, widowed, alone. I understand it completely because my life is like a winter's touch—desolate, empty, cold, and lonely.

Virginia's loss destroyed me. I was paralyzed in the accident. I would never remarry—who wants an invalid? My life ended when Virginia's life ended. I felt incomplete. Not only because of my legs but because Virginia was gone. I missed my other half.

An ambulance pulled up. Two guys jumped out and dropped a black bag beside the victim. The Jefferson's kid from across the street said something to the paramedics. They looked at my house and then at me.

"That sure is something, eh, Bry?"

I jumped. Well, half of me jumped—the upper half.

Captain Michaels stood beside me. When did he get here? And how did he stand on my lawn behind me without me seeing his cruiser?

"What's something?" I asked.

The captain grabbed the handles on the back of my chair. He pushed me toward the street. I wondered what he was up to but decided not to ask. Something about getting closer to the scene felt right. It'd been a long time since it felt this right. Just go with the flow. Let it happen. I wanted to get as far from my house as possible. Then maybe I'd be free.

"Must be lonely in that big house by yourself," he said.

I wasn't sure if this comment was in the weird category or the just plain rude department. He knew my circumstances better than anybody. I knew his. This was a small town. Everyone knew everything about everyone. I decided to remain quiet and not dignify that question with an answer.

Then he said four words that won the prize for craziest of all. As he pushed me away from my house, he said, "You'll never be free."

"What?" I don't know how or why, but a revelation was coming.

We hit the sidewalk's edge, and Michaels wheeled me onto the street. We were getting closer to the ambulance.

I turned away when we got close enough to see the body. I took pride in never being a rubbernecker. After seeing my wife's body in the carnage years ago, I'd never wanted to see an accident victim again.

"It wasn't my fault. It was an accident. I tried to get out of the way." The words slipped from my mouth, almost like they weren't mine.

Was I talking about the accident from many years ago? Did my guilt surface to form words?

I felt strange. Too much was happening without answers.

I finally looked at the man on the pavement. He bore a slight resemblance to someone I might've known. What got my attention was something I hadn't seen from my guest-room window. The man's pants were tied together above the knee, where he was missing the rest of his legs. Ten feet past his body was a busted-up wheelchair, just like the one I was sitting on.

Was I losing my mind, or was I looking at me, dead, in the street?

Captain Michaels tilted me back on the two large wheels, spun me around, and began pushing my chair toward my house. I turned back and stared up at Captain Michaels. It all hit me like an awareness, a consciousness.

Captain Michaels died six years ago.

He was the driver of the other car that careened into mine. Or did I turn into his cruiser? It seems foggy now and hard to hold onto.

When he pushed my chair up the ramp in front of my

house, I knew I couldn't be there anymore. I had to get out. That was why everything happened today.

I was dead and had been dead since my suicide two weeks after I killed my wife and Captain Michaels.

They had been having an affair.

I remember everything now. I had decided to die the day I found out. Then I thought it would be better to kill them, too. How brilliant is that?

The accident left me alive, sans legs.

Two weeks after being discharged from the hospital, I rolled my chair in front of a white Honda Prelude in front of my house.

I've been stuck here since, haunted by my dead wife and her former lover. Both of them enjoy their carnal knowledge in whichever room I'm not in. Both of them teased and taunted me until I let go and relinquished my sanity to them.

But I will not submit. I will not let go. I will resolve this somehow. They think they're haunting me, but I torture them every day that I exist here.

I turn back before passing the threshold of my virtual prison and see that the street behind me is empty. No ambulance, no accident, and no Jefferson kid is pointing at me. I imagined the whole thing. Or did they orchestrate it to torture me further?

Somehow, I know it's me trying to get out of the house, my feeble attempt at escape.

When I turn back, I see Virginia. After the accident, she always wore the face it gave her. A ghoul's mask that any self-respecting zombie would yearn to own. Her lower jaw is missing. Her nose sheared off. As she had turned away from the colliding cars, her face was only slightly angled to the left, exposing her right side to the dash. (I had removed her airbag the week before and mine to ensure the job was executed well).

Her right cheek was dented so far I could look up and see the back of her eye and the attached muscles. Her right ear had been shoved so far back that it dangled off the nape of her neck, attached as a ghoul's delight. Only the left side of her face contained any sense of her former self.

Whenever she smiled, I saw the three teeth she had left. This caused her words to come out in a whisper/whistle resonance.

"Dead again?" she asked.

"I will escape you one day."

She attempted to laugh. It was grotesque, her head back, her torn ear tapping her shoulder, still attached by small folds of skin.

Captain Michaels stepped around the chair and faced me. He'd been luckier. His airbag had deployed perfectly, hitting him squarely in the chest, saving him from all physical injury except one. The problem with Captain Michaels was his heart. When the airbag smacked him, it stopped his already frail heart, then burst it under the intense pressure, killing him instantly.

"These games you continue to play, they have to end," Michaels said.

I don't respond. There's nothing for me to say.

"You cannot kill yourself over and over in your head," Michaels continued. "That's no way to escape. From now on, you have to live in the basement. We won't tolerate this behavior, will we, darling?" Michaels looked at Virginia. She had stopped laughing.

"That's right," she said. "No more insolence."

I looked around for a weapon. I had to stop them. I couldn't live in the basement. The house showed itself for who it really was. The walls were falling apart, the floor collapsing. The front door sat open, a breeze swinging the screen back and forth.

What had my life become? What had I become? Was this all there was? No Heaven, no Hell? Just me, a ghost of my former self, haunted by people I once cared about?

They must have had some kind of hold on me, something I had to discover and reverse before I could escape their grasp.

But what was it, and how could I figure it out if every day was a repeat of the last?

Captain Michaels moved behind my chair and pushed me toward the basement door.

I heard a vehicle pull up out front. I had enough time to turn in my chair and look through the large bay window in the living room that looked out to the street. A van had stopped outside, the company's name emblazoned across the side: Rico's Demolition.

Demolition?

Did that mean someone was coming to tear down my house? If that was the case, would I be free then?

Frank shoved the chair hard at the top of the stairs to the basement. I tumbled out of it and fell down every step as I heard him laughing. At the bottom, I looked up and saw him folding my chair. He tossed it down after me, nearly hitting my head.

Just wait, I thought. *One day, I will get out of here*. When I do, I will kill you over and over. Whether they tear the house down, rebuild it, or leave it the way it is, I will find a way. I will torture you. If anyone moves into this house or a rebuilt version, I will terrorize them to ensure their house falls upon its foundation. One day, I will escape, and when I do, the world will never forgive you for what you've done to me.

Vengeance is mine, and pain is my ally.

I am the haunter, the haunted, and the haunting.

The Truth

Kramer Kay had volunteered, but it was against her will.

For events like these, she had a police escort in case anything came up.

When she studied the crowd of about two thousand people, she wouldn't just see them. She'd also see past relatives who stayed with them, people who were emotionally bound to them. Concentration proved difficult under these circumstances. Sometimes, a murder victim would show up and point out their murderer, or a past relative would reveal a secret that held legal ramifications. This kind of thing wouldn't hold up in court, but the police had made arrests in the past and had, after a thorough investigation, been able to formally charge others with various crimes.

She looked at the people meandering through the seating

arrangement at the Convention Centre in Toronto. It had a large crowd capacity for this type of conference, and the place was sold out for this evening's event.

Kramer's job was to answer questions from the audience. A lottery system was in place for all ticket holders. They were given a wristband with a number on it. A select number of participants would be called, and—when they heard their number—they would come to a microphone set up in the central aisle on the main floor and ask Kramer any question they wanted.

On the dais, Kramer tried to focus. Hundreds of faces stared back. Other faces floated by. She felt haunted, but without the Hollywood scary, evil that went along with that word.

Was it a gift or a curse? How often had she asked herself that since first seeing people on the other side?

Her first was her grandmother. She visited and played games with her for two weeks straight. Grandma told her stories about her childhood in the early 1900s. Kramer had been eight years old and hadn't been informed of her grandmother's death for over three weeks after the fact. Her mother had wanted the funeral and burial to be done first, but then the grieving was too great for her to talk about it. After three weeks, she'd been able to tell little Kramer about it.

"But she's not dead," Kramer had said. "She was just here."

"Kramer. That's no way to talk about the dead."

"But Mom, she just played *Monopoly* with me. And then we played Crazy Eights."

Her mother was obviously getting upset. Kramer could

tell her words hurt her mother but didn't understand what she'd done wrong.

"Kramer, I'll not have you saying such things." Her mother stood and walked away.

Kramer looked down at the carpet. "I'm sorry, Mom. Grandma told me about raising you and how you were in ballet when you were seven. I was wondering if you'd take me to ballet."

Her mother gasped, a hand covering her mouth. "How could you know that?"

Kramer met her mother's eyes. "Grandma told me, silly. I already said that."

Kramer's name being announced over the auditorium's speakers snapped her out of her reverie. It was her turn to take the podium. Wristband numbers were being called. Kramer was introduced and welcomed with applause.

She moved to the microphone, trying to keep her eyes cast downward, away from the prying stare of the dead. They almost always pestered her to find their living relatives if she made eye contact. Her purpose today was to help the living, not the dead.

The first few questions were about relationships. Would I ever get married? Can you tell me if my boyfriend is cheating? Am I destined to be happy? The answers went smoothly, and people sat back down, content.

The fourth random number drawn was a woman. She approached the microphone in the center aisle and asked about her son.

"I'm being told your name starts with the letter C. Is it Clarice or Clara?" The woman nodded. Kramer lowered her head and listened to the other side. "Your son passed away six months ago."

"Can you tell me if my boy is okay?" the woman asked, her voice altered by her emotions.

"He's happy. I'm hearing the name Jimmy. That was his name, right?"

Kramer focused on the woman's face.

A new bout of tears rushed from her eyes.

If the proverbial pin dropped, the thousands of people in the Convention Center would hear it. The quiet had become a character, only interrupted by a cough or a sneeze.

Kramer took a deep breath. "He says you always called him Jims. He wants me to tell you something. You're wondering what's happening to his Winnie the Pooh teddy bear. Is this true?"

The woman held the stem of the microphone so tight Kramer could see the white tips of her knuckles. An eerie-sounding yes was sent across the crowded arena. The woman hadn't said the word as much as she breathed it.

"Every night, he comes when you are asleep, sometime around two or three in the morning. He puts the teddy bear on his favorite chair. He wanted it to look like it was him sitting there. He feels the intense pain you're going through. At five years old, he didn't know any other way to express his presence to you."

A man stepped closer to the woman. He wrapped an arm around her shoulders as she leaned into him.

"Go home today knowing that Jimmy is with you. Remember that he lives on in your heart."

After a few minute break, more questions were asked,

allowing Kramer time to drink water and compose herself. When Kramer was down to her last ten minutes of stage time, at the end of a thus-far-uneventful session, she was startled to see an entity watching her from the side of the stage. She stopped in mid-sentence and looked to her right.

The most intense eyes stared back. The woman was from the other side, but something was wrong with her. She stood at an odd angle like she was reaching for something.

Before Kramer looked away, another woman materialized behind the first one, another pair of eyes, more intense than the last.

Kramer scanned the crowd to see who they were connected to. Two people remained in line. Kramer answered their questions and was about to be relieved from the stage when she asked if she could deal with one more problem. After such an astounding performance so far, the organizers were more than happy to let her continue.

The message she was getting from the dead women to her right involved murder.

She stood at the podium and surveyed the crowd once again. She needed to find the right people first and formulate a plan.

Would they have a gun?

Thirty seconds of silence passed before she spoke.

"We have a small problem here." She adjusted her shirt and glanced down at her feet. She was trying to figure out the best way to say it while also avoiding the eyes of all the entities watching her, now more intently than before. Looking back up, she glanced at the two police officers on the side. Both stared back at her, riveted by what they'd seen today.

She faced the audience.

"We all have people around us from the other side who have passed over successfully. But there are others who don't pass over. They are what we call earthbound, most commonly known as ghosts. It seems like they haunt us, but actually, what they're trying to do is get our attention. They don't know they're dead yet. They see you, but only on rare occasions can you see them. We feel and hear them more than we see them. Almost all ghosts haunt a dwelling like a house or a building—a location that ties them emotionally to this plane. All earthbound entities are here because of some extreme emotional attachment." She inhaled deeply, then let it out slowly. "At this time, we have an entity with us which is not haunting the conference center. They're stuck here, on this plane, because of someone in the audience."

Kramer continued to study the crowd. "I was just told the name because I can hear the earthbound entity whispering it repeatedly. Could Norma"—Kramer paused, trying to hear the last name better—"Jenkins, please rise and come down to the microphone."

Everyone in the building turned or leaned forward, searching the pavilion for movement. Who was Norma Jenkins, and where was she?

Wherever Norma was, she remained seated.

"Norma, we need to talk about this. We need to help the people on the other side. No matter what they did here, leaving them earthbound is like having them in limbo, a form of purgatory. I feel so much pain coming from this woman, your mother. Her name is Gertrude Jenkins."

No one moved. No one stood.

Kramer looked to her right. Four women were standing there now. She looked at the woman in the front and followed her eyes to the floor seats. If the murderer knew he or she was being revealed, who knew what they would do? The murderer—whoever they were—brought a weapon tonight, according to the whispers of the dead.

"I'm here to help," Kramer said. "You don't need to be afraid. Please come to the podium and tell me what has caused you such grief."

A woman stood, her gaze locked with Kramer's. She started out of her row and walked down the aisle, making her way to the microphone.

She tapped it twice, then said, "My father is dying. When he was diagnosed with cancer three years ago, my mother left him. I can never forgive her for that."

Kramer slipped her hand in her pocket and pulled out a lighter. She lit a candle on a table beside the podium and held it up.

"Your mother died two months ago, Norma. Haven't you wondered why you have those nightmares since? The ones where you always dream of murder."

She glanced at the two cops again. They were both still there. A collective gasp rolled across the audience.

Kramer continued. "You've been curious about what's causing this, and I'm here to tell you that it's your mother. You're very connected to her. The sorrow you're dreaming of is her pain."

Norma scrunched her face and narrowed her eyes. "Are you saying my mother was murdered?"

Kramer looked away, straining to hear more. "Your mother left your father. She had to. He was abusive. He was also caught in compromising situations. Your mother had enough. Two days before she moved out, he sprang his illness on her in hopes that she would stay. But she saw through the hoax—"

"What hoax? What're you saying?"

"Your father doesn't have cancer. He never did. If you hurry, you can ask him yourself before he leaves."

Norma turned around to look where she'd been sitting and saw her father sliding along the seats. When he got to the aisle, he turned and stared at her. Because Norma's mouth wasn't as close to the microphone, the crowd had to strain to hear her ask her father if this was true. Everyone saw him lower his head. He turned away and walked out of the conference building without answering her.

Norma looked back at Kramer. "My mother tried to tell me," she paused to pull out a tissue. "She called and called, but I avoided her. Dad said his cancer was in remission and how much he missed my mom. Oh, this is bad. I guess I shut her out so completely that I forgot she was there. I'm sorry. I'm so, so sorry. Can you tell my mom that ... wait." Norma stared at Kramer. "You said something about murder."

"I'm sorry, but your mother is earthbound because she was murdered." Kramer looked at the two cops again and motioned for them to step closer.

"How come this is the first I've heard of it? They ruled it a suicide."

"That's this man's MO. He is methodical and knows what the police will look for."

"How would he know that?"

Kramer felt her stomach twist. How could she get the murderer arrested without too much trouble? She didn't think it would be possible. By now, the man knew he was the one she was talking about. She had to watch closely. He might even pull out his weapon and try to shoot her. He was standing ten feet from her, and his victims had grown to six entities now. They all glared at him with an intensity that grew by the second. If she concentrated hard enough, she could see where each murder took place and how he did it. All that would be needed later to aid in the investigation, but right now, she had to make sure the murderer didn't leave the building.

"Because he's a cop," Kramer blurted before she could caution herself.

There was a collective gasp across the stadium. A member of the psychic committee that had invited her walked over and touched her arm. "Okay, I think that's enough now."

Kramer yanked her arm away. "Don't you dare bring me here, ask me to use my gift, and then try to quell me at the first mention of trouble or people feel uncomfortable." She turned to the two police officers only six feet away and pointed at the one on the right. "Officer Hank Denton is a murderer, and I can prove it. Arrest him."

Hank turned and ran, already pulling his weapon out of its holster. His partner yelled after him, but it was too late. Hank hit the opening between the bleachers and disappeared.

"You better be right about this," the other cop said.

The sound of a gunshot resounded throughout the

building. Instantly, Kramer stepped back to the microphone.

"Everyone stay seated. Remain calm. Everything is all right now. If you've trusted me thus far, trust me now. We're all going to be okay. Do not leave your seats. I repeat, do not leave your seats."

At least thirty percent of the crowd had started to rise, but slowly, one after another, they began to take their seats again.

The officer who had warned Kramer had pulled out his weapon and moved toward the exit. Everyone's attention remained focused on the man in uniform, walking toward the door where a gun had just been discharged.

The door cracked open before he got there. The cop lowered into a shooting stance, his gun raised at the person entering the complex.

Norma's dad stepped in, a gun in his hand, aimed at the floor.

"Drop it!" the cop ordered.

Norma's dad searched the audience for his daughter. "I'm sorry," he shouted. "It's all my fault that your mother was killed. If I had been a better husband—"

"Drop it. I won't tell you again," the cop said, his voice booming across the stadium.

He gestured toward Kramer on stage. "I was pretty sure it wasn't a suicide. But I'm no cop. How could I ever find my wife's killer? When I heard you say it was that cop, I had to, I just had to."

"Last chance to drop your weapon," the officer yelled at him.

An alarm sounded in the building somewhere.

Norma's dad opened his right hand and let the gun fall to the floor. The cop ordered him to the ground. He had cuffs on him in seconds.

The audience clapped like the whole thing was a performance set up for their entertainment.

Kramer looked at the six dead women. They were dispersing now, moving to different parts of the auditorium, and their intensity diminished.

Emotionally spent, Kramer stepped away from the microphone and left the stage.

When she heard the siren in the distance, she decided to wait to give her statement. The sooner, the better.

She could explain what had really happened.

She felt terrible for having lied to Norma. Her mother committed suicide. Kramer had been told that Norma's father really did have pancreatic cancer, with only about six months to live. He also had a gun because he'd been severely depressed over the loss of his wife and had entertained the idea of killing himself to be with her. Norma's family situation was the best fit for what Kramer had to do to out the cop because he wouldn't have stopped unless he'd been arrested or killed. As far as Kramer could tell, he'd murdered eight women and gotten away with it—all had been deemed suicides. According to the other side, he planned on killing more than another dozen women before being stopped. They helped her formulate the plan to involve Norma's dad, as he was armed. The only way to involve him was to pretend that Norma's mother was part of it.

Norma's dad killing the cop really made no difference to him, as horrible as that was, because he'd be dead long before any sort of trial would take place. Although that act saved the lives of all future victims, she deemed it a necessary evil.

She'd been offered a glimpse of his future, the cop's deadly record, the whole story, and acted as best she could.

Then why did she feel so bad when she literally just saved the lives of so many women?

"I hate this job," she muttered under her breath.

She picked herself up and went to make her statement.

Déjà Vu

I'VE BEEN FOLLOWING THEM for over thirty minutes on the highway, and I'm starting to think they're onto me. The driver is passing vehicles recklessly, increasing his speed as if trying to lose me. But I can't allow them to get away, or people will die.

I first saw them at a truck stop, eating lunch. Looking at them, I had a strong sense of déjà vu. At least, that's what I call it because people understand what that means.

My events are much different, though.

When I'm in the grip of my type of déjà vu, I feel it, see it, and know what will happen the second it does. The major difference is that everything I sense during my déjà vu always happens one hour later than the second.

This one happened at 12:10 p.m. That means at 1:10 p.m. I will go through the emotion of someone regaining their memory. An explosion will take place, and a life will be spared. That's what I saw at 12:10 p.m.

I don't know whose life is in jeopardy or what the remembering thing is all about, but I know it has everything to do with the people in the Nissan Pathfinder ahead of me.

My cell phone in my breast pocket startles me. I yank it out, watching the Nissan and my speedometer. The display says it's my wife. This isn't good. I'm supposed to be home by three p.m. I won't make it home any time before six now.

"Hello?"

Shit. Why did I even answer the phone? I could've called her back after the incident was dealt with.

"Hi, honey, how long before you're home?"

"Ah, sometime around six tonight." I can't lie to her.

"Why so late? What are you doing?"

"It's difficult to explain."

The Nissan pulls out and passes a hatchback. A small line of rigs is coming my way up ahead in the distance, so I can't pass yet.

"Are you acting on one of your déjà vus again? I thought we talked about that. You weren't going to do it anymore."

"This one's different. It's more personal. If I don't resolve this one, someone will die."

I'm right behind the hatchback now, waiting to pass. Vehicle after vehicle is coming from the other way. I can see the Pathfinder is gaining speed, getting away from me. I have to do something. I have to get off the phone and focus. Time is running out.

"You said you'd ignore those episodes from now on after almost getting yourself killed climbing onto the roof of that office building."

"I know, I know, but I saved that woman's kid, didn't I?"

The Nissan Pathfinder turns a corner up ahead and disappears. I look at the dash clock: 12:57 p.m. I have thirteen minutes to get them in my sight again and be close enough to experience the déjà vu in real-time, or a disaster will be on my conscience.

"You didn't know for sure that she would throw her kid —"

"Look, I gotta go. I'm sorry. I'll see you when I get home." I flip my cell shut and toss it on the seat beside me.

I come around a bend in the road, and the Nissan is at least a mile ahead now, about to be lost from sight again as it dips below a hill.

1:02 p.m.

I don't understand what's happening. Because it's my déjà vu, I have to be there. I saw it happen. This means I was there to see it. But I have only eight minutes to catch up, which doesn't seem likely now.

There's a break in oncoming traffic. I have a small enough opening to pass, but now the hill where I lost sight of their vehicle is looming, and I can't make it around any vehicles without placing myself in danger.

I gun the engine and pull out to pass anyway. The top of the hill is coming too quickly. I can't see over it yet. If someone's coming, neither of us will have much chance to avoid a head-on collision.

The timing couldn't be worse. My stomach drops as adrenaline shoots through my body.

A dump truck crests the hill. The hatchback I'm trying to

pass is directly beside me now.

There's no time to finish passing him. I jam on my brakes, and to my horrified astonishment, the hatchback driver does the same. He must've thought to let me in, as I was passing anyway, but now we're slowing down, side-by-side.

The dump truck driver leans on his horn, smoke rising from his rear tires as they're locked.

Everything is happening too fast. Everything's based on instinct—there's no time to think now.

I hop to the left onto the oncoming traffic's gravel shoulder at the last instant. Whether that's instinct or a strong sense of self-preservation, I'm grateful for the move as it saves my life.

The dump truck—which didn't have ample time to stop or take evasive action—shoots between the hatchback and my car.

Collision averted, I ease back onto the pavement as we crest the top of the hill, my heart leaping in my chest.

The road ahead is empty. The hatchback driver motions for me to go ahead. He must figure he'd better let me go if I'm desperate to pass him.

1:07 p.m.

I drop the accelerator to the floor and try to get my breathing under control. My hands are shaking on the wheel. The rush of almost having a head-on collision with a dump truck oozes through my veins.

I race around the next bend in the road with only minutes left. Two police cruisers are parked on the shoulder. The Nissan Pathfinder I was following is sitting just ahead of them. The male driver and his female passenger are talking to the officers. As I get closer, I can see a tripod on the shoulder of the road. The police have a radar trap set up, and it looks like they've stopped the Pathfinder for speeding. I've got a minute and a half left.

A light starts flashing on my dash, indicating engine trouble. Well, I'm pulling over anyway.

When I stop and park, the Nissan driver is pointing at me. I open my car door and head toward them, looking in all directions for the potential danger I'd seen coming.

"He's the one who was following us," the driver shouts. "Every time I would pass someone, he would do the same."

A police officer faces me. I look at my watch, fully prepared to act on the déjà vu, although I have no idea how to act. I just know someone's life is at stake. I have no idea how big the explosion will be or where to hide. I just know it's all coming.

Before the cop says anything, I shout, "Everyone, move away from the road's edge. Do it now!"

No one moves. The cop walks toward me, gesturing. "I'd like to have a word with you."

I hear a crackling noise behind me. I try to turn around, but at that moment, my car explodes, knocking me off my feet.

I lose consciousness in the air.

***

My wife's voice comes to me. Someone's holding my hand. My eyes must be moving under their lids. She let go of my hand, called for someone, and told them I was waking up.

Ten minutes later, after a welcomed sip of water, the doctor left, and my wife told me that I'd been out for three days. The media are calling it a miracle.

"How is it a miracle that my car blew up and I'm in a coma for three days?"

"The car exploded from a leaky fuel line. If you had left that truck stop on the highway where you were having lunch and started for home, which was over two more hours of driving, the car would have exploded with you in it. They still don't know why you were following the Nissan, but they speculate it was because of the woman."

"We both know why I followed that vehicle." I watch her face, my mind swirling with how close I came to dying. "The déjà vu."

"That doesn't matter. I would never tell them about your episodes. They wouldn't believe me anyway. But this time, you saved your own life."

I remember one of the things that came to me at the truck stop. A life would be spared. It all felt so personal. Maybe a part of me knew I was going to die. That part that sees others' futures must've seen my own and orchestrated everything to save itself. Amazing.

"What was that about the woman?" I ask. Then I realized she must have something to do with my feelings about someone remembering something. "Did she recall what it was she was supposed to remember?"

My wife takes a moment to respond. I see her eyes well up with tears.

"What's wrong, honey?"

"I'm a sucker for happy endings," she says. "You really did it this time."

"Did what?"

"The woman traveling in the Nissan Pathfinder got hit in the head by flying debris. When she was admitted to this hospital, she told the authorities she'd forgotten her real name. It turns out she was kidnapped over five years ago. They rarely deal with things like this. The authorities brought in a specialist from Toronto. One of the cops told me yesterday that the woman had been subjected to years of sensory deprivation. The driver of the Nissan had convinced her he was her husband. At first, they thought she was a victim of Stockholm Syndrome, where she felt sorry for her kidnapper. But then they realized she actually believed this guy was her husband."

"Are you serious?"

"The woman was reunited with her real husband and two kids just this morning. You should have seen it. Her children are only seven and nine. She told them she had amnesia and …" My wife stops to wipe her nose. "She lost over five years with them. It's such a tragedy."

This is the biggest déjà vu mystery I'd experienced. It's also the scariest. Will I have more of them?

My wife blows her nose and composes herself. "Please, do something for me. Act on every feeling you get because today, my husband is my hero."

A déjà vu hit me in that second.

The man who kidnapped the woman was arrested and made bail this morning. He's on his way here to find out how I knew, and he aims to kill me. In one hour to the minute, I see him throwing me out the hospital window and making it look like I jumped—suicide.

I lift off the bed, the pain in my head and back screaming for me to stay down.

"What are you doing?" my wife asks.

"We have to leave the hospital. If we don't, we'll both die. Help me up. Do it now."

Her face turns beet red, her composure challenged by my brusque tone. But to her credit, she reached over and helped me out of bed.

The door to my room opens.

The driver of the Pathfinder steps in.

"What are you doing here?" my wife asks him.

It's too late. He's here. He'll grill me for an hour and throw me out the window. My déjà vu only covers what'll happen in an hour, not what gets me there.

I lean back onto my bed and say, "I'll tell you how I knew."

I feel my wife gasp. The man steps closer to my bed. He has a weapon in his hand.

"Start talking," is all he says.

"It's déjà vu."

I have to convince him I can see the future. If I can do that, then I will tell him that I see him dead in one hour and the only way to escape it is to leave before the police get here.

He raises his gun and shoots my wife, the gun making a soft spitting sound.

I have never felt the way I feel when I see the look on her face. Then she falls to the hospital floor below the side of my bed.

"I don't care how you figured it out. I came here to kill you and your wife. After that, I will throw you out the window. It'll look like a murder-suicide."

In all this, I cannot believe my brain is still working. "Wait," I gasp. "If you kill me, they'll know."

"I'll wound you so you won't try to escape, but not bad enough to kill you. Like this." He raises his weapon and fires.

A bullet tears into my side. I scream. He's on me in a flash, covering my mouth and silencing my voice.

"It'll look like you killed her, tried to shoot yourself, and then tossed yourself out the window when you failed."

My hospital door opens and then closes. No one enters.

He turns my gaze to the door and then down at the floor where my wife had fallen.

"Shit!"

He releases his grip on my face and runs. I know that my wife got away. He hits the door and slips out.

An alarm sounds throughout the floor.

I'm bleeding. Losing consciousness.

I sure hope my wife makes it. For both our sakes.

I'm passing out from blood loss …

Thoughts

Jack Singer's time on death row for the murders of Mary Edell and her husband Ralph was soon to come to an end. It'd been four long years with no appeals. Jack recalled that night quite well. He'd cut himself while carving the Thanksgiving turkey. The jury had found him guilty as his blood, his DNA, was found at the murder scene.

The real killer would have worn gloves. The real killer would have been careful.

Jack's wife and son had been out of the country visiting relatives, but Jack had stayed behind, and Ralph had invited him over for Thanksgiving dinner.

He was an innocent man. His wife knew it. However, the justice system convicted him and sentenced him to death by lethal injection, which was still practiced in the State of Texas. The only thing that could save Jack in his final hour was a stay-of-execution call from the governor's office, which didn't seem likely.

The door to his cell clicked into the unlocked position, announcing his hourly check-up. Security performed these checks to count all death-row inmates, making sure that none had escaped or done harm to themselves.

A guard stepped into his room and shut the door behind him. Jack felt something was wrong right away. The guard's mannerisms were different and odd. The guard's eyes jostled back and forth. He hunched over as if his back was giving him trouble and repeatedly looked at the cell door. The first thought in Jack's head was drugs—the guy was either high or drunk.

"Jack, you're going to be okay," the guard whispered. "I know you didn't do it. You will be going home to your wife and son shortly."

What was this guy saying?

Whatever he was up to, hearing someone feel Jack was innocent wasn't comforting. It was too late for that. To absolve guilt, a whole new trial would have to take place, which didn't fall under the category of "shortly."

"What I mean is," the guard continued. "I'm not going to let them hurt you. God resides on the other side, but today, God is on your side."

"What are you talking about?" Jack finally asked.

"I was sent to make things right. I'm here for you."

The guard turned for the door, stepped out into the corridor, and locked Jack inside.

He wouldn't allow himself to hope. Not at this late hour. Today was his last day. Everything was in place and had been in place for a long time. One security guard couldn't do much.

Jack turned from the door, mentally dismissed the guard as a whack job, and sat on his bunk to think about his family. He hoped they wouldn't show. The last thing he wanted was to have them remember him this way.

***

Five correctional officers escorted Jack to an area with ten holding cells. He was being received in this new area from the Ellis Unit before execution.

One of the five officers was the guard who had visited Jack earlier with his crazy talk about Jack being freed shortly.

The hunched-over guard winked at him. Jack wondered about the guy's sanity but didn't say anything. The guard looked capable, confident, and well put together. He must be at least six foot three, even with his shoulders slouched. It was obvious to Jack that the man worked out quite a lot, the uniform stretching around his biceps. He decided to call the man Mr. Odd, as his behavior matched the moniker.

Jack turned his thoughts inward to focus on his family in the time he had left. It saddened him that he would never see his son grow into a man. It broke his heart that two good people were dead, and everyone thought he was the one who killed them. But most of all, Jack felt destroyed on the inside that he wouldn't get to grow old with his wife. Even though he had tried to prepare for this mentally, he felt crippled by it. He'd gone through all the stages of grief: denial, anger, bargaining, depression, and acceptance. He was going to die.

There was nothing else left except prayer. His last silent prayer was for a call from the governor. Jack might get out of jail one day if he'd grant a stay. It may be a long time, but at least there was hope if the stay was granted.

Mr. Odd glanced at Jack. "There's always hope, my friend. Have faith, Jack, have faith."

The other guards looked at Mr. Odd, confused.

The clearances had come through from the governor and the attorney general. It was time to move Jack to the execution chamber. He was placed on a gurney and secured by leather straps around his wrists, biceps, chest, stomach, and legs. A saving grace was they hadn't put a mask or a hood on him yet.

Intravenous tubes were set in, one in each arm, and a regular saline flow was started. After the speakers and microphones were checked, the witnesses were brought into the execution facility. At times, he fought to keep his dinner down. He broke out in a sweat as people were being ushered in to watch him die.

With thoughts of his wife and son racing through his mind, he kept saying to himself, *don't show up, don't show up*.

Not two minutes later, he saw his wife with his son.

Why would she bring their child to witness this?

In a crazy move, taking Jack completely by surprise, Mr. Odd reached over his body, obstructing his view of the people outside the windows, and yanked Jack's IV lines out of both arms.

He winced at the sharp pain, but since Jack was strapped down, he couldn't twitch or move to cover the small wounds.

The guard pulled out a concealed revolver and told everyone to leave the execution chamber. It all happened so fast. One moment, he looked at the people arriving outside the chamber, and the next, he was a hostage inside the chamber.

The guard must have strong feelings toward Jack's innocence—so much so that he'd just gotten himself into a lot of trouble.

"What are you doing?" Jack asked.

"Everything will be fine. Trust me, just trust me. Tonight, it'll all come clear. Then you can do the work you're supposed to be doing."

People were shouting at Mr. Odd, telling him to put the gun down. Jack looked around as best he could in his restrained position and saw that the guard still held his gun up, aimed at the door. Jack saw him look at his watch.

"There," the man said. "That should do it. I only needed to delay this procedure for ten minutes. I'll see you later, Jack."

The guard set his gun on the floor and kicked it into a corner. He raised his hands in surrender and stepped from the room.

Moments later, new guards arrived and announced the execution procedure was being put off temporarily. Jack was removed from the gurney and led back to his holding cell.

An hour went by before a minister entered Jack's cell.

"Hello, Jack. I have come with news."

"What news?" Jack asked.

"The execution has been stayed."

Jack was flabbergasted. "What do you mean, *stayed*? Why?"

"The governor just called to stay your execution because DNA found at the farmhouse was filed in error, and they have a confession. It has now been matched to a man who has similar convictions and is, at this moment, sitting in a jail cell pending a hearing on a separate murder charge. Apparently, he confessed to the murder of Mary and Ralph not two hours ago, thinking you had already been executed. But something else is quite weird."

Jack sat down hard. He didn't care what was weird and what wasn't. He knew he'd die if Mr. Odd hadn't stepped in. Jack had been told that the entire process of lethal injection takes approximately seventeen minutes from start to finish. Mr. Odd had held the procedure up long enough to save Jack's life.

"What happened to Mr. Odd?" Jack asked. After seeing the confusion on the minister's face, Jack shook his head and said, "I mean, the security guard who stopped the execution."

"No one knows."

"What do you mean, no one knows?"

The minister paced the floor. "They'd put the guard in a holding cell until charges could be filed against him, and when they went back, he was gone. They'd even posted a guard to watch the cell. A camera has videotaped footage of the door to the cell. No one left the room after they put him in it. They've asked around, and apparently, no one had ever seen the guy before, either. He's a ghost, a myth. He disappeared. It seems like someone was looking out for you, Mr. Singer. It looks like God was on your side today."

Jack lay back on his cot and wept. What really happened? Would he ever find out? The guard had been right:

Jack was being released soon. He could go home to his wife and his son. He could try to resume his life after losing so many years on death row. They'd have to move, relocate. People would still judge him, but he was alive when he should be already dead. There were so many plans, so many things to think about now that the weight of death had been lifted from his shoulders.

The minister was just shutting the door.

"Wait," Jack called.

The minister stopped and poked his head back in. "Yes?"

"You said something was quite weird. What did you mean by that?"

The minister looked up and down the corridor and then stepped back into Jack's cell.

"I heard, and mind you, this is unofficial, that the guy they arrested for the murder you almost died for not only confessed, but he also said he had to do it. He had been given instructions. He said the plan was all laid out for him. The goal was to have you executed, and convinced as he was that you were already dead, he started talking."

Jack was taken aback. "Why? I mean, who would do such a thing? Who could orchestrate something like that? Why would they?"

The minister shrugged. "He's staying mum on who supplied him with the how and when, but according to his confession, he said the reason was because you were evil. You did Satan's bidding."

The minister crossed himself.

"Satan's bidding?" Jack laughed. "And how would I have done that?"

The minister watched him sideways. He opened the door and stepped back out into the hallway.

"Jack, you don't have a son or a wife. You were never married."

The minister shut the door hard. It is locked from the outside.

"No one understands," a voice behind him said.

Jack jumped and slipped off the bunk, hitting the floor on his ass.

"How did you get in here?"

Mr. Odd stood in the corner using a toothpick to clean his teeth. Jack could see the smile on Mr. Odd's lips. As his lips spread apart, his eyes did, too. The farther his mouth opened, the face followed. It gave him an altogether strange countenance as if his face were made of rubber.

"I come and go as I please. Now, we have business."

"We have business? What does that mean? They said I'm free, I'm out. I am leaving to go see my family as soon as they give me my walking papers."

Mr. Odd laughed. Jack looked away. The sight of the thing's face was suddenly too much to handle.

Maybe I've been alone too long?

"You're fine, Jack. This happens sometimes. You'll get used to it."

The minister's last words still echoed in his mind. I don't have a son or a wife? How could he say that?

"It's easy." Mr. Odd stepped closer. "It's a simple trick of the mind. I tell them what to think. Until I remove the implanted thoughts, they'll always think whatever I want them to."

Jack edged away and leaned against the wall of his cell. "I have no idea what you're talking about. No one can do what you claim. And if you're so good at owning thoughts, then why did you have to pull a gun to save me from lethal injection back in the chamber?"

Mr. Odd shook his head. "A collective mindset is dangerous. I can do it one by one, but that many at one time is not good. Even for me."

"Have you changed my thoughts, my memories? Do I have a family, or is the minister the one who has it wrong?"

"You do have a family." He nodded. "You can go back to them. But first, we have business. Until our business has been concluded, people will assume you don't have a family. Even your wife doesn't know you anymore. It was funny. You should've seen her face. Why am I here? I must be morbid. I don't want to see a strange man die. Oh, she is a riot."

While Mr. Odd laughed at Jack's wife's actions, all Jack could think about was getting away from him. He had grown to accept his fate months ago, but in the last few hours, he was told he would live. He would be able to grow old with his wife. He could raise his family now. The black cloak that had become his life had been removed. It was over, and this thing before him was talking about business. He had no business with Mr. Odd. At any time, guards would come and release him from jail. His wife would pick him up, and all would be right with the world again.

Mr. Odd shook his head in the negative. "I don't think so."

"You don't think so what?"

He stood, his massive bulk even bigger than Jack remembered. The room smelled like decaying meat mixed with old yogurt.

"You don't understand. The man who confessed only thinks he did it. Everyone here has been told the right information. None of them are my pawns. But your wife and son don't know about you anymore. Once you agree to do what I ask, in return, I will—"

"You bastard." Jack had heard enough. He lunged at the monster but missed and smacked into the wall. When he spun around, Mr. Odd was smiling again.

"I wouldn't do that. You'll never be able to touch me unless I let you."

Jack pushed himself off the wall and dropped onto his bunk. "What now?" he asked between breaths. "Even if I were to believe you, what now?"

"There's a man I need to be killed. He's a vile person. You'd be doing the world a favor because some people should die. After you complete this task for me, you get your life back. All planted memories of all parties will be erased. Everything goes back to normal. Are you agreeable?"

"I can't kill a man. I never have, and I never will."

"Ah, but you're forgetting what I am."

"How's that?" Jack asked. *How long before guards show up to release me?*

"Don't worry about the guards. They won't come until we're done our little talk."

"How do you know that?"

"If I can change memories and thoughts, don't you think I can read them, too? Come on, you're a smart man."

He felt acute fear for the first time since Jack met Mr. Odd. Was there a safe play here, an easy way out? Could Mr. Odd be real, or was this some kind of sick joke?

"As soon as the deed is done, you return to your wife, and she'll wake up looking forward to seeing you. Your life will go back to normal."

"The alternative?"

"You leave here and never see your family again for as long as you live. You'll also look over your shoulder for the rest of your life as you'll never know when I will have someone think that you are to be terminated."

"Your negotiation skills are superior," Jack said, his nose clogging with the stench coming from Mr. Odd. Decay appeared to be rapidly changing his features. "Is something happening to you?"

"I can only hold form for short periods. Make a choice, Mr. Singer. I'm running out of time."

"Okay, I've made my choice."

Mr. Odd nodded for him to continue. Part of the skin on his cheek slipped off and plopped onto his shoe.

"Pray tell."

Jack had no idea where he was anymore. He looked down at his fingers as they twitched above his knees.

"I refuse to do anything whatsoever for you. I am a man who was on death row. Another man has confessed to the murders that I did not commit. I am to be freed to go home to my family. Whoever, or whatever you are, is an abomination. There is no way what you're saying can be true."

He looked back up to gauge Mr. Odd's reaction, but he was alone. Jack stood and looked around. In seconds, the decaying meat smell dissipated.

"Oh, good," he said to himself. "It's over. He's gone."

The door lock clicked, and then it opened. The minister from before stepped in, five guards standing behind him.

"Are you ready?" he asked.

"Sure. I cannot wait to see my wife and son. They're going to be happy. Oh, wait," he leaned closer to the minister and, in a lower voice, said. "You know I have a wife, right?"

The minister stepped back and looked at the closest guard. "Yes, Mr. Singer. I'm aware that you're married."

"Perfect. That little charade is over. Well, let's get to it."

He stepped out and turned to the right, but the guards blocked his way.

"It's this way, Mr. Singer."

"No, that way is the chamber. I'm free. The call came in. The guy confessed, remember?"

The minister looked at each guard, and then all six men stared at Jack.

"Are we going to have a problem here?" the lead guard asked.

"Why would we have a problem? I'm free. There was a confession." Jack's nerves couldn't take any more.

"There's no confession, Mr. Singer. Your execution didn't receive a stay. The audience has reconvened. Everything is on time. Please come with us. Don't make it hard on yourself."

"Wait, what about the guard who took a gun out and stopped the injection? You remember." He turned to the minister. "You and I just talked about the confession not half an hour ago."

"I'm sorry, Mr. Singer. I have no idea what you're talking about. There has been no guard with a gun, and this is the first we've talked today."

Jack turned and ran but was quickly subdued.

He caught a glimpse of Mr. Odd standing at the end of the hallway, smiling.

The Wallet

I WOULD NEVER HAVE believed this story if you told it to me. Yet, there are moments in our lives when opening our minds can allow miracles to enter. You wouldn't hear me utter those words two months ago. Something happened to me which has no explanation. Something akin to a mystical event. I would even go so far as to say I've been touched by someone or something from the other side.

I'm a very particular person. My friends call me a perfectionist. My home is neat and in order. I can tell you where everything is at any given time. I've always had a mental running inventory of my condo and workplace. I don't do this on purpose. It's just the way it is. If someone uses the stapler on my desk at work, I can tell it's been used by how they set it back down. I don't go out of my way to study the position of everything—I just know when it's been moved. Maybe it's an OCD thing.

Most of us have a certain amount of this eccentricity. With me, it's turned up a notch. That's why I'm a good cop, which got me my current job as lead police detective. Could it be I have a photographic memory?

The point is I rarely lose things. I have never lost a set of keys. I have never, ever lost money.

I have never lost my wallet.

But on May 7, 2009, something happened that I can't explain.

My wallet disappeared.

When I say disappeared, I mean magician stuff. It actually vanished. And because it did, lives were saved.

That day was a long one for me. It was a Thursday, and I was in court all day—it goes with the job of being a cop sometimes. Anyway, I need paperwork after that and then back to my condo. With more work at home, I walked the six blocks to my neighborhood coffee shop for an eleven p.m. beverage.

I grabbed my wallet and keys and headed out. The air was crisp, the walk rejuvenating. I needed a break, and this was it.

When I got there, it wasn't too busy at the counter. The staff had just changed the shift at eleven p.m., so the two-night girls were peppy and eager to serve.

I got my coffee and left, walking along the side of the building to the back parking lot, where I skirted past a couple of parked cars. I was halfway through my coffee when I got to the main entrance of my building.

That was when I noticed my wallet was gone. Impossible

was my first thought. It couldn't be. I checked every pocket. I looked at the ground around me. I tried to remember if I'd taken it for this walk. Then I recalled opening it to pull out a five-dollar bill to pay for the large coffee. My hand found the coins in my front pocket to confirm I'd used a five.

Maybe I dropped it on the way home. Although, I don't know how that could be.

Is it still sitting on the counter in the coffee shop, lost to the first set of devious hands that find it?

There wasn't more than a hundred dollars in my wallet. The problem wasn't money. It was the identification. Having to replace all of that would be a nightmare.

I retraced my steps with eager speed. Block after block, I hustled back toward the coffee shop. My heart seemed to beat faster and faster the closer I got. Every possible solution went through my mind. Were they holding it for me at the counter? Did a stranger have it and was just now charging electronics to my Visa?

I tossed my empty cup into a trash can in the back parking lot. I jumped off the back curb and almost got hit by a car. A four-door Malibu, burgundy in color, raced by me not a foot away. He was going too fast for a coffee shop's parking lot. It was almost midnight, and the lot had two cars in it. He missed both but couldn't negotiate the turn around the large square dumpster. I watched in awe, my wallet dilemma temporarily forgotten, as this guy hit the dumpster doing at least seventy to eighty kilometers per hour.

The airbags deployed, knocking the driver back in his seat. I raced over and leaned in the window to check for a pulse. I found one, but it was weak. The driver was unconscious, his nose bleeding. No one else was in the car. I reached for my cell phone and realized it wasn't there. I'd left it at my condo.

The driver was wearing gloves. The non-bacterial kind you'd wear when handling someone with a contagious disease.

Also, the kind you wear when you don't want fingerprints left behind.

My internal radar activated. I scanned my immediate surroundings. I was alone with the driver. After ramming the dumpster, no one came out of the coffee shop's back doors to check on the car's noise.

Could this be a getaway car?

I started for the back door of the coffee shop. The door stood ajar, light seeping out onto the darkened pavement.

Someone shouted something about a mistake as soon as I got there.

"Ramos was a mistake. We shouldn't have used him. I knew he'd panic."

The speaker couldn't have been twenty feet from me. I entered the back of the coffee shop and was greeted by one of the bakers sprawled out on the floor. He had his hands on his head.

When he saw me, he gestured wildly to get out. He used his right hand to point at the door, jamming it like a mime, trying to tell me the building was on fire.

I mouthed the word cop and continued toward the front of the restaurant.

"Did you hear me?" the voice from a moment ago yelled from the front area.

I heard this just before the last turn that would lead me to the front counter. As luck would have it, my mind was working at peak performance thanks to the caffeine in the large coffee I had just bought and drank from this very café.

The perp wasn't on a cell phone. He was talking to someone in the building.

My head spun around to face the baker sprawled out on the floor.

He wasn't on the floor anymore.

The bad guys always herd the hostages into an area where they can be watched. They would never leave a baker by himself in the back room. I should've caught on to that. Now, the baker was gone, and the back door opened wider than when I entered. He must've hightailed it when I told him I was a cop.

"John, you okay back there?"

I moved forward and took the last turn that put me directly behind the front counter. The perp was by the tables with the two female night staff and a couple of male customers. My advantage was that he didn't know his baker accomplice was gone, so I stood, grabbed a donut, and bit into it.

I said, "Ever since they introduced these blueberry fritters, I haven't been able to stop eating them."

I had everyone's attention. The perp held a knife. He did a half turn, not wanting to completely take his eyes off the hostages in front of him, his mouth agape in surprise.

"I know they're just like the apple fritter," I continued, "but these babies have a blueberry filling." I held it up for everyone to see. I took a second bite as I walked around the counter's edge and stepped within six feet of the perp.

"Who are you?" he stammered.

"Police." I bluffed the rest. "Your driver is in my cruiser. Your baker accomplice is in cuffs, and you're in trouble."

A siren wailed in the distance. I waited for the right moment. The creep looked out the window where his car should have been.

I threw the rest of the donut at him.

He reacted when the donut hit him by thrashing the air with his knife, which I expected. I slid on the floor like I'd hit a good ball into the right outfield and was sliding into home base.

I connected with his legs, taking them out from under him, and spun sideways to avoid having his body weight land on me when he came down. Within seconds, I had the knife knocked out of his grasp, and his arm wrenched back far enough to be able to control his movements.

I kicked the knife away and looked outside to see two cruisers pull in. The on-duty officers took it from there.

And then the craziest thing happened.

When they took my statement, the officer wanted to see my identification and badge number. I reached into my pocket and pulled out my wallet. I stopped and stared at it. He asked me if everything was okay. I told him everything was fine without telling him why the wallet held meaning.

As I said before, I have never lost a wallet. Was it there the whole time? Or did it disappear, and when its purpose had been served, it returned?

Whatever happened to my wallet that night will remain a mystery forever. All I know is that its little performance made me return to that coffee shop, which was crucial at that exact time because a robbery was taking place.

Who knows what would have transpired if I wasn't there?

Who knows where my wallet went for thirty minutes on the evening of May 7, 1999?

Sounds like magic to me.

Afterword

DEAR READER,

My journey with religion (or call it a belief system regarding something of a higher power) began in the frightful days of my youth during Sunday school sessions with angry nuns.

When I was six and seven years old, my brothers and sisters and I were bussed to a school setting where tall women dressed in black shouted a lot and carried long yardsticks that they enjoyed smacking things with—think desks, walls, hands—always with enough vigor to create a sharp noise. They taught us about the original sin and how man must suffer their entire life after being tempted by a woman, who must also suffer after being tempted by a snake.

It was explained to me as a young child that I was sinful due to being born and that unless I accepted Jesus into my heart, I would burn in a lake of fire for eternity. Since I was so young and didn't know the first thing about the Bible yet, I asked who this man named Jesus was (because my mom would often shout his name when she stubbed a toe or burned a finger). I won't recount the trouble I got into and the promise of eternal Hell for speaking in such a way. The tears I wept that day were for the soul. They told me I had forsaken in the name of one of God's angels, some dark guy who had fallen somewhere.

Ultimately, my parents took us out of Sunday school because their children came home in tears every Sunday.

Fast forward to 1984, when I was fourteen years old.

In January, my brother froze to death after being lost in the Alberta mountains.

This made me want to learn more about God. I wasn't questioning His existence. I just wanted to talk to Him or be heard by Him. So, by sixteen years of age, I was in Bible study. My parents disagreed with it then, but I continued the lessons regardless. The Old Testament was hard to endure as God sounded malicious and egotistical. Believe in Him, or you'll be punished, sort of stuff.

In the New Testament, God seems to have calmed down with his punishments and slowed his public appearances.

So this led me to research the Bible and how it became the King James version. I also researched some of the translations from the original Hebrew. In the end, I discovered that the current Bible we ascribe as the Gospel has many interpretations and ideas as to what it initially said.

Finally, this led me to visit churches and try to learn or examine religion. I started with Pentecostal, but after a few visits with an entire church speaking in tongues and not explaining why or what they were trying to say, I moved on to Calvary Baptist. When they told me that the "believe in Jesus or go to Hell" bit was alive and well, I asked what happened to all the human beings before Christ's time—I mean, how could they believe in someone who hadn't even existed yet—and it was explained to me that they are all in Hell.

What about the African aboriginal tribes discovered in the past fifty to one hundred years? Are they in Hell, too?

According to the leader of the church I visited, they are. They were doomed if they hadn't heard of or accepted Jesus into their heart.

For me, that couldn't be a God of love.

So, I moved on to Mormons and others and continued learning, absorbing as much as possible.

I spent my twenties researching God. I read book after book on religion with titles such as *How to Know God* by Deepak Chopra and *A History of God* by Karen Armstrong, to name a few.

This led me to New Age religion and studies on the other side.

Life After Life by Raymond Moody blew me away. *On Death and Dying* by Elisabeth Kübler-Ross was also a moving example of the other side and the power of emotion to bind us on this plane and the next.

In the late 1990s, I decided to write a book on religion and all I'd discovered in the past 15-20 years of research.

The result was these short stories.

I wanted to show the world that God is love and that

there is another side when we leave here (in my opinion). This isn't a statement of fact, nor am I encouraging or attempting to convert anyone into believing what I believe. That would be ridiculous and grandiloquent of me.

I'm simply coming to a conclusion that led me to where I am today.

Which is that I'm a believer.

I may not believe in this God or that God, but I do believe in a God.

And whether we want to discuss reincarnation, damnation, or Adam and Eve versus the Big Bang Theory, in the end, I think there's a God behind it all.

I also believe our souls live on.

There's been too much proof from near-death experiences (NDEs). Too much has been seen by nurses attending the near-dead in hospices to have *nothing* beyond our curtain-of-life stage.

My dead brother inspired the Sarah Roberts Series because he came to me in dreams and told me about the future several times. These things came true, and I was amazed by how it happened.

I've lived in a haunted house where there was knocking on the walls and things moving throughout the night. I lived there with my first wife, who can attest to these strange occurrences nightly.

I later learned upon moving out that there had been a murder/suicide in that haunted apartment years before. When the apartment was vacant, neighbors often heard fighting and screaming from the empty dwelling. (This haunted house inspired a short story in the other collection I wrote called

Don't Shoot).

I've seen, read, heard, and been involved too much *not* to believe.

And once I wrote these stories, plus a few others lost forever, I began the Sarah Roberts novels in earnest.

The rest is history.

Thank you for reading these stories that date back to the 1990-2000 era.

Some of the other short stories I wrote are in *Twisted Fate (Tales of Horror)*, which are in the same vein as these but lean more toward the horror genre.

In the meantime, I'll get back to work on more Sarah Roberts novels. I hope you're all doing well and staying safe.

Keep in touch with me on social media, and most of all, keep reading.

Until next time, take care of yourself and each other.

Blessings,

Jonas Saul

About Jonas Saul

Jonas Saul is the bestselling author of the Sarah Roberts Series—more than two million sold!—and has written and published over sixty thrillers. After acquiring an agent, he signed several deals in Los Angeles, with MadRiver Pictures optioning his Sarah Roberts Series— over forty books!—(currently in development).

Jonas has often outranked Stephen King and Dean

Koontz on Amazon over the past decade. He's regularly invited to be a guest speaker, teacher, or workshop presenter at international writing conferences and film festivals worldwide. He hosts an annual writer's retreat in Greece, where he currently lives. He focuses his teaching on how to get tension and emotion in every scene, on every page, how he made it as a creator/writer, the path to success in this business, and the pitfalls to avoid. He also hosts a reading retreat in Greece with guest authors, yoga retreats, and hiking retreats. Visit the Imagine Greece Retreats website at www.imaginegreeceretreats.com, or email him directly to discuss an opportunity to join one of the retreats at jonas@imaginegreeceretreats.com.

Jonas is also a professional freelance editor. He works for several publishers and does private editing for clients, with many testimonials on his website at www.imaginepress.org, which details each author's response to Jonas's editing skills. Email Jonas directly for an editing quote at editor@imaginepress.org.

To book Jonas for a speaking engagement at a writer's conference/festival, to have him on your jury at a film festival, or even to say hello, email Jonas directly at jonassaul@icloud.com.

For updates on releases, hit the "Follow" button on Amazon or Bookbub, and join Jonas on Facebook, where he's most active.

Contact Jonas Saul

Linktree: Find me here

Email: jonassaul@icloud.com

* 9 7 8 1 9 9 8 0 4 7 9 2 5 *